SPERMJACKERS FROM HELL

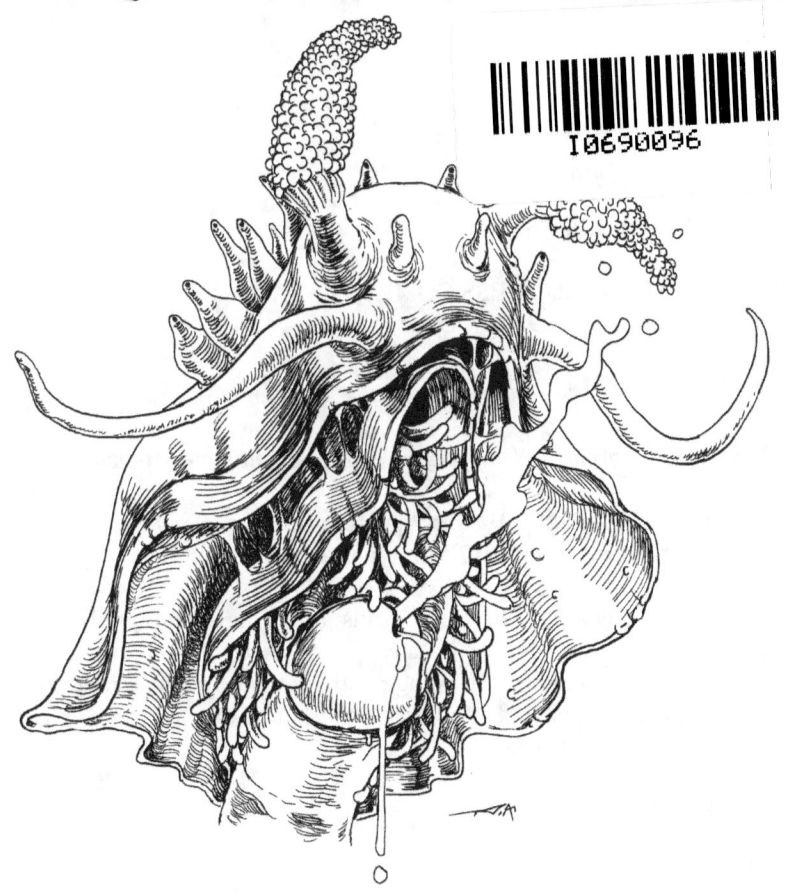

I0690096

CHRISTINE MORGAN

deadite press

deadite
press

DEADITE PRESS
P.O. BOX 10065
PORTLAND, OR 97296
www.DEADITEPRESS.com

AN ERASERHEAD PRESS COMPANY
www.ERASERHEADPRESS.com

ISBN: 978-1-62105-247-0

Spermjackers from Hell copyright © 2017 by Christine Morgan

Cover art copyright © 2017 Jim Agpalza
Interior art copyright © 2017 Jim Agpalza

Printed in the USA.

For my family ... especially my daughter Bex,
who I know is just so proud,
whose friends will be so impressed,
and who will never be able to live this down,
ever.

"Let's summon a succubus, he said. It'll be fun, he said."

"Shut the fuck up!"

"*You're* the fuck-up!"

"*Both* of you, shut up already!" Jake strafed Marty and Spencer with an auto-fire glare, of which Devon—who hadn't made a peep—caught collateral damage.

It worked, though. They did shut up. Or maybe it had more to do with Marty needing to bend over and catch his breath with his hands braced on his knees, while Spencer backed into a corner, covering his face like a little kid at a scary movie. Except, most little kids, when backed into a corner covering their faces, probably wouldn't keep silently mouthing a litany of fucks.

Being down here...being chased this way...hunted this way...it'd be a miracle if either of them made it out.

If *any* of them did, for that matter.

Devon wasn't too wild about their chances. All he wanted was not to die down here. To not end up like those others they'd seen...

"I think we ditched them," Jake said. Whispering, like it mattered what with Marty huffing and puffing and gasping and wheezing.

"Great," said Devon. "So, where *are* we?"

This time, it wasn't auto-fire glare but a single sniper-shot, with nothing collateral about it. Devon flinched. He hadn't been trying to challenge Jake or piss him off; he honestly had no idea.

They'd been scrambling around this claustrophobic labyrinth for what felt like hours, sometimes with nothing to go on but the pale shine of cell phones, sometimes groping through blackness in a terror of giving away their position.

And sometimes, worst of all, in the eerie, shimmering, blue-green gleam of...

Shuddering, Devon forced himself not to think about that.

He raised his phone—how much longer on the battery? He didn't dare check, because he knew the news would be grim. The wan light made them all look like post-apocalyptic

5

infected maniacs. The disheveled state of their clothes didn't help, nor did the bruises, scrapes, and scratches on their skin. But they still looked miles better than they could have, all things considered. Compared, to, say, the unlucky ones. Or, what was left of them. Okay, so, maybe the hobos hadn't been in the best shape to begin with, maybe had barely looked human and alive when they were up and moving around, but still...

He tried to shake the images from his mind but they came back like mental pop-up ads. Their faces were the worst. Their expressions. Their horrible, hideous, dead faces.

Well, their faces were the worst he'd let himself look at. He hadn't been able to bring himself to look...lower.

Again, with a physical headshake to go with it this time, he tried again. Not going to think about that. Not going to see that in the shadow-scape of his mind. Not now. Not ever.

Except in nightmares, but, for there to be nightmares, he'd still have to get out of here with body and soul together.

Right now, the four of them were alive, relatively unhurt, and still mostly fairly sane.

If Jake was right with his "think we ditched them," they might be able to stay that way a while longer.

"I just mean," Devon said apologetically, "you told us you knew your way around—"

"Forget it." Jake turned away to listen. "Yeah. I don't hear anything."

"Jesus fuck," Spencer said, sagging into his corner. "Jesus H. Titty-Fuckin' Christ. I was sure as shit we were dead as shit."

"Oh, man." Marty mopped his face with the bottom of his GTA t-shirt, showing a view of hairy gut Devon could've done without. Not that he hadn't already seen way more of everybody than he'd ever wanted. "Can I puke now?"

"No puking," Jake said. "We've got enough problems."

"Those bodies back there—" Devon said.

Spencer held up a palm-out. "Don't, or Mart-O here won't be the only one pukin'."

"But—"

6

"Spence is right," Jake said. "Don't. Like I said, we've got enough problems."

"Okay, okay," Devon said. "You *do* know where we are, though, right?"

"We'll figure it out."

"You mean we're lost?"

"He doesn't mean we're fuckin' lost!" Spencer shot to his feet. "We been down here a bunch of times, Jake and me, and we're not—"

"Shhh!" hissed Jake.

They fell silent, Spencer snapping his yap closed, Marty struggling to control his breathing. Devon, his mouth dry, tried to swallow and heard the rasp and click loud inside his own head. He heard the quick thump of his heartbeat, an irregular echoing drip from somewhere, the faint scuffle of a what might have been a rat or cluster of roaches…and nothing else.

Nothing else.

The tension began to ebb from Jake's shoulders. Marty loosed a shaky exhale that turned into a sour burp. Spencer mouthed a few silent obscenities of relief.

False alarm. Only a false alarm. Maybe Jake was right.

"Are we—?" Marty began in a hoarse whisper.

"I think—" Jake's words cut off.

A low sound rolled in like ground-fog from the stillness. A throaty chuckling. A murmuring, a rustling. Feminine. Seductive. A sound made to curl around nerve endings and caress senses. To entice with promises of pleasure, to stir memories and desire.

"Oh, fuck," said Spencer.

"Move it." Jake grabbed Marty's elbow and propelled him past Devon, then turned to hoist Spence from his corner.

Marty stumbled, almost faceplanted, recovered, and began to run in a heavy, lurching lumber. Devon, Spencer, and Jake followed, hoping to find something, anything. A dead end would be bad. An exit would be good.

Instead, they came to an intersection, where Spencer stopped short and moaned in dismay. "You gotta be shitting me."

7

"What?" Marty mopped his face with his shirt again. "What now?"

"We been here before."

"What?!"

But there was no denying it, as they shined their phones for a better look. If the familiarity wasn't enough, the fresh snack cake wrappers were a surefire giveaway. They *had* been here before. Now, their hectic scrambling had brought them back, and what Devon couldn't remember was which way led out...and which led toward...

The lair, something in his mind suggested.

He shuddered.

The den. Come into my parlor said the spider to the fly.

No, thanks.

Slip into something more comfortable.

Stop it.

You're so tense, you should relax, relax and think nice things.

It occurred to him that nobody had moved, all four of them just standing there, as the brightness of the screens weakened into milky blurs.

Won't hurt you wouldn't hurt you you'll like it it's nice.

Sure, tell that to those hobos.

Devon shuddered again. He shook himself. "Guys!"

Spencer jumped. Jake blinked. Marty went, "Huh?" Then awareness dawned on each of their faces, awareness with dread hot on its heels.

"Still after us," Jake said. "And close."

"So let's get the fuck gone!"

"Yeah, but which way?"

Jake's eyes bugged, and for a second or two, Devon thought he was finally going to crack and abandon ship on the whole big-balls leader routine. Which way? Screw that, every man for himself! If they each took a different direction, hell, maybe some of them might make it!

Then the no-man-left-behind one-for-all-all-for-one mentality set in again, and Jake found a sudden decisiveness. "This way!"

Swearing, Spencer took off after him. Groaning, so did Marty.

Devon hesitated for an awful moment, half-convinced they were now heading full-speed right toward their doom. But, if he didn't follow, he'd get left behind. If he got left behind, he might never get out. Gripping his own phone tight in one clammy-sweat-slick hand—no bars, no service; useless as anything but a light source and even that was fading fast—he broke into a run.

Stay it's nice love you love you make you happy make you feel so nice so happy and nice warm and relaxed and pleasant and nice.

It was wrong.

It all had been wrong.

Wrong from the start. Wrong as a joke, as a just-for-the-hell-of-it, just-for-the-fun, when none of them seriously expected it to work.

Wrong to get involved. Wrong to go along.

Any pretense at stealth was abandoned as they ran, change jangling in their pockets, the soles of their shoes slapping with flat echoes, phone displays bobbing and casting weird streaky glimmers.

A joke, for the hell of it, just for fun.

Why hadn't they done something else?

Why hadn't they listened to Beth?

Forget her forget her she doesn't see you know you love you understand, she can't make you happy can't make you feel nice not like this not like us not like me so much better so much much much better.

Stronger now and closer. Too strong and too close.

"We've got to buy some time," Jake said.

"How?" asked Devon.

"You *know* how."

"Shitfuckfuckshit." Spencer cupped his hands to his crotch. "I can't, sincerely, my dick hurts, I can't."

Marty laughed. It was a terrible, un-funny laugh. "I'm running on fumes, here, bro."

Their three faces, awash with shadows, all turned toward Devon.

"Who, *me*?" he yelped.

"Somebody's got to!" said Marty.

"Yeah, go on, get with the fuckin' program and *do* it already!"

"Jesus, Dev," said Jake. "Take one for the team, huh?"

What we want, what you want, what I want, what we want, you'll like it it's nice.

It wasn't in Devon's ears but between them, not in his mind but below it, a thrumming undercurrent to thought and reason.

Horrible.

Beautiful.

Promising pleasure.

Incomparable, irresistible, unbearable pleasure.

"Hey! Fuck yeah!" Spencer suddenly cried. He'd pulled into the lead, the wiry rat-bastard, overtaking Jake, outdistancing Devon, leaving Marty lagging in his dust. As the others drew nearer, they saw what he was pointing at.

"Ohthankgod," panted Marty.

"Told you it was this way!" Jake managed a grin, regaining some of his swagger. "Let's get out of here."

"Fuckin' A," Spencer said.

Get out, yes. But then what? Who would believe them?

That could wait. Discussion later. Anywhere but here.

They hadn't gone half the distance toward the beckoning beacon, the promise of salvation, when the sounds reached them again. Murmuring, chuckling, rustling, a low and intimate whispering.

Feminine sounds, sounds to sway and stroke and seduce. Cooing and crooning.

Sleek. Terrible. Supple. Sexy.

None of them spoke. Spencer didn't bother to swear. They just ran again, ran like hell, ran like rabbits, ran in a headlong panicked final sprint.

As, behind them, clear blue-green gleams appeared, rippling shimmers of sun-on-tropical-shallows turquoise, an enticing and intoxicating promise, wonderful wet warmth, and a shining, deadly, hellish hunger.

10

Before...

CHAPTER ONE
INSPIRATION

"Dude," Marty said to Brendan, tearing open a pillowcase-sized bag of Doritos. "I keep telling you, you're wasting your time going after tourist girls."

"The fuck would *you* know about wasting time, Mart-O?" countered Spencer. "You been trying to Nice Guy your way into Cynthia-Lynne Abbott's pants since sixth-fuckin'-grade."

"I have not!" He flushed.

"You totally have," said Beth, leaning forward from a swaybacked old junker plaid sofa to snag herself another beer.

"Who's Cynthia Abbott?" asked Devon, who'd only moved to Fairmont a few months ago when his parents decided to try their luck opening a little bakery/bistro, and remained very conscious of his status as the new kid in their circle.

"Cynthia-Lynne Abbott," Marty said, with a quickness and emphasis that only proved Spencer and Beth's points. His flush darkened toward maroon.

"Blonde," said Spencer, an expression of busy rodentlike concentration twisting his narrow face. Dried green makings and papers were strewn on a card table in front of him as he rolled with industrial assembly-line precision. "Not much for tits, but legs like holy-Judas-whoa."

"Dude!"

"What? They are."

"They are," Jake said.

"I'd give her a seven, maybe an eight," Brendan said.

"Poor Mart-O could only give her about a three and a half," Spencer said. "If he ever got the chance, which he won't, on account of she's stuck his ass so far in the friendzone he needs a goddamn passport."

Marty threw a chip at his head like a nacho-cheese ninja star and missed by a yard. It skittered off somewhere into the apartment's general litter and clutter.

"She's dating Troy Cahill," Beth told Devon.

"Of Cahill Cellars?"

"Who the hell else?" Brendan said. Sounding bitter, and with good reason. His parents made money, yeah, sure, but they weren't Fairmont-elite. And if *Brendan* was bitter about such totem-pole bullshit, the rest of them weren't even in the running. Jake's job at the golf course paid okay but was seasonal, Marty's at the Shop-N-Go was strictly crap hours and minimum wage, Beth did part-time at the lock shop, Devon's folks had all they could do to keep their heads above water, and Spencer...

Hell, Spencer was a Bodean, which said it all.

"That jerk," Marty said. "I don't know why she keeps going back to that jerk." His thumbs blurred across the controller. On the screen, a dozen gibbering yellow-eyed demonic imps exploded in a succession of gooey black and red bursts.

"Because he's Troy-fuckin'-Cahill of Cahill-fuckin'-Cellars," Spencer said.

"He doesn't appreciate her. He doesn't deserve her. She's always saying how insensitive he is."

"Tell us again how you're not Nice-Guying," Beth said.

"I'm *not!*"

"Girls say stuff like that," said Jake, popping some frozen corn dogs into the microwave. "They say they want someone who's smart and funny and considerate—"

"Yeah!" Marty blew away more imps and a rotting cadaverous thing dripping acidic ooze. "They *say* that, but then they go for assholes like Troy-fucking-*Cahill*! Won't even give someone decent a *chance*! Whoa, shit!"

A larger demon, this one a greenish behemoth sporting huge bone horns and scythelike claws, had appeared in the passageway. Its maw opened in a huge, screen-shaking, but near-silent roar. The volume was turned way low because the guy in the unit next door—a behemoth himself, with shaved head and neck tats—had informed them in a deceptively soft, polite voice that he worked odd hours and would appreciate it if they kept it down. Needless to say, nobody argued.

"Banefire spell," Beth said.

"I know, I know, shut up, I know!"

"Another one behind the rubble."

"Aaargh!"

The gaming chair rocked and shook as Marty lunged side to side, death-grip on the controller, leading with his elbows. A ball of sulfurous flaming energy shot from his avatar's gauntlet, stunning one demon before he swung around to engage the other.

Several violent seconds and a couple of extremely close calls later, it was over. Jake clapped Marty on the arm. "Nice save, there, man."

"Hate those horny bastards," Brendan said.

Exhaling, fortifying himself with a big swig of his Mega Guzzle, Marty relaxed and picked up where he'd left off. "This one time, at some party, they got into a big fight, and he ditched her, and she called me, and I walked her home—"

"Was that the time she puked on your shoes?" asked Beth.

He nodded, watching as two sections of wall crumbled to reveal a fiery chasm spanned by floating chunks of jagged stone bobbing at irregular intervals. "Yeah. She was really drunk, crying, upset. I held her hair and everything."

"All that, and you didn't even get a blowjob." Spencer tutted. "Sucks for you. Or, should I say, *no* sucks for you."

"Anyone else would've tried something," Brendan said.

"Hey..." Marty finished traversing the fiery chasm by jumping across the floating stones in the correct pattern. "... I'm not the kind of scumball who'd take advantage of a half-passed-out girl!"

"That's good, though, right?" said Devon.

"You'd think," said Beth.

"And how'd she thank you for it later?" asked Jake, in the tone of one who already knew the answer.

Marty's shoulders slumped. "She told me I was a really—"

"—*great friend*," Jake, Spencer, and Beth finished with him, and he sighed.

"We gotta get you laid before you die of terminal blue balls, bro," Brendan said. "It's getting embarrassing."

"I'd say, hire a hooker," said Jake, "but, a., you make even less than I do, and b., a guy has to have *some* pride."

"Yeah," Marty said. "Sometimes I wish they'd hurry up and make with the Japanese sex-robots already."

"Not that you could afford one of those, either." Beth rolled her eyes. "Maybe Spence can get you a discount with his cousin over in Winston City."

"Hey, Jolene's a slut, not a whore, there's a fuckin' difference." Spencer paused, chuffing out a chortle of smoke as he considered his words. "Well, the fuckin' part's not the difference. But Jo ain't no ho."

"They do make those robots pretty good now, though," Brendan said. "I've seen them on the internet. Really lifelike and detailed. Customizable. You can order them however you want. Some porn stars even have licensing deals."

"Classy," Beth said.

"But with a *robot*?" said Devon. "I mean...how?"

"Ah, fuck, if we gotta have the birds and the bees talk with the new kid, I'm gonna need more weed." Spencer picked up two more joints, lit both, and sent them into circulation.

"Cut scene, cut scene, everyone shut up, this is the good part!" Marty said, waving for their attention.

The swirling darkness on the screen diffused to reveal a cavern of pale limestone formations, seething rivulets of blue-black gaseous liquid, billowing emerald flames, and an immense throne hewn from rock crystal.

Throngs of servile, groveling imps scampered aside as a statuesque figure arose from the throne. A curvaceous, wasp-waisted, inhuman, scantily-clad, and *extremely* top-heavy figure.

Llylth, demon queen of the hell-sluts, approached with languid, hip-rolling strides on shapely legs ending in polished, tapered hooves. Her barb-tipped tail swayed like a cobra in a snake-charmer's basket. Folded wings more suedelike than leathery trailed from her shoulderblades.

"Fuckin' A," Spencer said, with an appreciative leer.

The camera angle on the cut scene panned slowly around, depicting the demoness from above, behind, below, and in extreme close-up. A lot of time and effort on the part of the animators had gone into every painstaking detail... some details far, *far* more than others.

Brendan wolf-whistled. "Let's hear it for boob physics!"

"Yeah, that's *soooo* realistic," Beth said.

Jake laughed. "A diabolical hellscape where it rains poison fire, damned souls roaming around with their guts hanging out, and her boobs are what you call unrealistic?"

Marty shushed them.

With a voluptuous slow-motion jiggle, Llylth raised her arms to unclasp a gold chain from around her neck. The close-up fixed on its pendant—a glowing bauble filled with writhing smoky female silhouettes like the opening credits of a Bond film—as it was languidly drawn out of her canyonesque cleavage, sending ripples undulating through demonic flesh.

Llylth dangled the pendant in front of her face, shown in profile as she spoke. All ripe and sensual mouth, lush lips parting, tongue curling enticingly. It looked prehensile, and forked.

"What's going on?" Devon asked. "What's she saying?"

"Turn it up, Marty," Jake said, quickly adding, "Not too loud though."

A voice flowed from the speakers, rich and sumptuous, a voice like a decadent dessert, something thick and creamy and probably alcohol-soaked.

"Mila Kunis," Beth said, as Llylth described how the power of the Amulet of Succubus Summoning could be invoked, to call forth her handmaidens. "Wait 'til you hear the Dead Lord. They got that guy from that one show, what's his name, Sheldon."

The cut scene ended with the demon queen giving the amulet to Marty's gruff, buff, chisel-chinned hellslayer avatar, informing him he could use it only six times…to assist him in battle against the Zephilim angels…or tend to other, more worldly, desires.

"You get different achievements depending on how you use it," Marty explained, as the loading screen came up. "The Zeffies are tough, so, a succubus really can save your ass in some of the fights—and the boss battle, against the archangel, is a *serious* pain—but I heard, if you don't call any of them until the room past the gate he unlocks, then call all six, you get another cut scene…a demon orgy."

"Shit, really?" Jake sat up straight. "I didn't know that! Have you done it?"

"No. Never been able to take down the archangel solo."

"Aw fuck yeah," breathed Spencer, exhaling a pungent cloud. "That's what we need, you guys. Forget hookers and Japanese sex-robots. We need an amulet of succubus-summoning!"

"Yeah, right," Beth said. "Because that's *always* a good idea."

"Think about it, though." Jake leaned back, gazing at the ceiling. "Your very own demon love-slave."

"What do they look like?" asked Devon.

"In the game?" Marty opened his inventory and highlighted the amulet, which popped up an image. "This is their natural form. You know, little bat-wings, tail, devil-horns—"

"Mostly naked, all tits and ass, total raging nympho," Spencer finished. "I'd do her."

"Me, too," said Brendan, ogling the scarlet-skinned centerfold doing a posed revolve on the screen. The succubus was not so much dressed as ornamented, in barbaric-looking hellgold jewelry and 'armor,' *a la* those old paintings by Boris Vallejo and Frank Frazetta. "Who wouldn't?"

"Well, *I* wouldn't," said Beth.

"Why not?" Jake grinned. "She's got a tail. She could do you with her tail."

"Funny."

"Hey, she could do *me* with her tail, I wouldn't mind."

Spencer took a deep drag and said, in a raspy held-breath croak. "Ass in the air like you just don't care."

"You gotta admit," said Marty, "it *would* be pretty awesome."

"Getting done up the butt by a demon chick's tail?" Beth asked.

"Not that part!"

"Speak for yourself," said Jake.

"They're psychic shape-shifters, too," Marty said. "They could turn into whoever you wanted."

"Yeah, forget customizeable robots," Brendan said. "A psychic shape-shifting nympho, that's some infinite variety right there."

"Your own personal demon love-slave." Jake inhaled deeply and held it, savoring.

"So, let's do it," Spencer said. "Let's try. Let's summon us a succubus."

CHAPTER TWO
PREPARATION

"Okay, so..." Jake consulted a sheaf of printouts. "For the pentagram, we'll need black wool twine, a shitload of salt, colored chalk, five flat silver plates, and five white candles."

"Shouldn't be too tough," said Brendan.

"It also says we'll need a...brass bell and a glass chime."

"Brass bell, where the hell do you get a brass bell?" Spencer asked.

"My mom has a glass windchime hanging on the balcony," Devon said.

"Great, bring that. For twine, I guess they just mean yarn, yeah? And a basin of pure water. Then, with a censer..." Jake paused, brow furrowing. "What's a censer?"

"When they don't let you say 'fuck' on TV," Spencer said.

Beth elbowed him. "No, dumbass, it's one of those swingy incense things priests use in church."

"Like I go to fuckin' church?"

"Let's see." Jake ran a finger down the paper. "Inscribe the ward-lines and sigils as shown, yeah, yeah...silver dish and candle at each star-point, okay...sound bell and chime with each struck flame...cast the smoke..."

"When do we get the hot naked demon chick?" Brendan asked.

"This is still setting up. There's like ten pages of instructions here."

"Seriously?" asked Marty. "I thought this was supposed to be the quick and easy way!"

"Hey, you could just tell Cynthia-Lynne Abbott how you feel about—" Beth said.

"Keep reading, Jake!"

"I'm not seeing where the yarn has anything to do with

it…hang on…okay, here we go, after you set up the candles on the silver plates, you string it around them to follow the ward-lines."

"I don't know, you guys," Devon said. "It's getting pretty complicated, and we're not even to the real summoning part yet. Maybe we should forget it and—"

Brendan made clucking noises.

"Hey, no, I'm not scared, I'm only saying—"

"Where we gonna do this, anyway?" Spencer gestured around the small and cluttered apartment. "Fuck, we'd have to clean first if we tried it here."

"What's your lease say about devil-worship?" asked Beth. "What about pets? Does a demon love-slave count as a pet? Your landlady would have a fit."

"We're not doing it *here*," Jake said. "Never mind the landlady; I'm not going to be ringing bells and chanting at midnight with a neighbor who already wants to turn my face inside-out if I shut the door too hard."

"Where, then?" Brendan asked. "And don't say my place."

"Mine, either; my parents aren't too sure about you guys yet," Devon said.

Beth smirked. "What, they think we might be bad influences?"

"Fuckin' parents, I tell ya, man," Spencer said. "Like they never smoke or drink or summon sex-demons."

"How about Coach's house?" Marty suggested. "He's cool."

"Not *that* cool," said Brendan. "He'll let us bring beer over but not weed."

"And, he already thinks women are fuckin' evil in general," Spence said. "You've heard him. No way he'd be for devil-women."

"We're not doing it at Coach's, either," Jake said. "Nobody else involved. Now, quit worrying about where; I've got a couple ideas. But there's going to be some other stuff we need, for the actual ritual, and it might get tricky."

"Like what?" asked Devon.

"Well, for instance, one hen's egg—"

"Big whoop, an egg," said Brendan. "What's so tricky about that?"

Jake held up a hand. "Needs to be freshly laid."

"Don't we all," Marty muttered.

"Will be, once this works," Spencer told him.

"Can someone get a damn fresh egg or not?" asked Jake, patience fraying.

"Sure, sure, chill," Brendan said. "There's this organic farm-to-table co-op my parents go to—"

Spencer smacked his forehead with the heel of his hand. "Jesus fuck, organic farm-to-table, ten bucks for a half-dozen, those fuckin' co-op hippies! Just give *me* the money; Nana Nell keeps a bunch of ratty-ass chickens, and I'll bring you all the eggs you want."

"Okay, so," Marty said, "eggs are covered. What else?"

Coughing a bit, Jake said, "The, uh, moon-blood of a nubile maiden."

"The what?" asked Devon.

"Eew." Marty grimaced.

Brendan glanced at Beth.

"I will punch you square in the throat," she said, without even looking his way.

"I didn't say anything."

"I will punch you square in the nuts, too."

"This is one fucked-up scavenger hunt," Spencer said.

"See?" said Devon. "Complicated. Maybe we *should* forget it and—"

"Don't give up yet, we'll figure something." Marty turned to Jake. "What else is on the weirdo shopping list?"

He hesitated, scanning the pages. His eyes widened a little. He coughed again. "Aw, just a couple more things, no big, we can handle it."

Nobody seemed fooled or reassured.

"Say it," said Brendan. "Just tell us already."

"Well...okay...it calls for a lock of virgin's hair..."

There followed a very awkward and uncomfortable pause in which gazes shifted, feet shuffled, eyes were averted, and a few more coughs were coughed.

"... and a virile youth's new-spilled seed."

"Dude," said Marty.

"Gross," said Beth.

"How new is 'new'?" Brendan asked.

"How new do you think?" Jake retorted. "Or were you planning on swiping some from your dad's spank-bank?"

"Who needs bottled and frozen when we got unlimited on tap right here?" Spencer did an extravagant crotch-hiking motion.

"Yeah, but, who's gonna..." Marty couldn't even bring himself to say the rest, making a feeble but familiar gesture with one loosely-curled fist instead.

"Like you said, we'll figure something," said Jake. "Anyway, that's it. Draw out the pentagram, provide those items, recite the words, and there you go."

"So, no, like, sacrificing a goat?" Devon asked.

"No, like, sacrificing a goat."

"Cat? Person? Baby?"

"No, no, jeez. It isn't that kind of spell."

"It's a *demon*-summoning spell," Beth said.

"Yeah, but, it's not that kind of demon, is it?" argued Brendan. "Not the kind to slaughter your enemies or whatever."

Marty eyed the book with renewed interest. "What do those kind need?"

"Oh, stow it, you don't have enemies," Beth told him.

"What about Troy-fucking-Cahill?"

"He's not your enemy, dipshit."

"Rival, then."

"Rival, my butt. He'd have to know who you even goddamn *are*."

"He knows who I even goddamn am!"

"Yeah," said Spencer. "His girlfriend's bitch."

"Anyway," said Jake, "for making the actual sacrifice, this one website says you can get away with using like crickets from the pet store, or brine shrimp, you know, Sea Monkeys. Even yogurt, because it's got living bacteria in it."

23

"Oh, hey!" Brendan suddenly sprang to his feet. "I know just what else we need!"

"Your heads examined?"

He ignored Beth's remark. "Where's my keys? I'll be right back."

"Dude," said Marty. "Are you cool to drive?"

"Always, bro, always!"

The door banged shut. Jake braced himself, but no noise from the neighboring unit meant they might've lucked out again. Footfalls thudded on the exterior walkway and down a rickety flight of stairs, shortly followed by the rev-and-roar of an engine.

"He is *such* a douche," Beth said. "*Why* do we hang out with such a douche?"

Spencer twitched a bony half-shrug. "'Cause he's a douche with money."

"And a car," Marty added.

"Why does he hang out with you?" Devon asked.

"Why do *you*?" Jake asked right back at him.

He winced. "I didn't mean—"

Beth laughed and opened herself another beer.

"We're just fuckin' with you, new kid." Spencer passed Devon a joint.

For a change, he took a few shallow but actual puffs rather than waving it on and only basking in the plausible deniability of second-hand highs from the permeated air.

"Mostly, Brendan's stuck hanging out with us because the Fairmont wine-snobs think they're better than everyone else," Jake said.

"But, aren't his parents doctors or something?"

"Or something," said Marty. "Not, like, medical doctors."

"So, like, what, then? Psychiatrists? Scientists?"

"They knock up rich bitches and charge them out the ass," Spencer explained.

Devon blinked. "They huh-what?"

"They run a fertility clinic," Beth said. "For couples who have trouble getting pregnant. Some people think it's kinda skeevy."

"Oh," he said. "So that's what you guys meant by his dad's spank-bank."

"Oughta just ask a Bodean." Spencer hitched extravagantly at his groin again. "Never been a problem for us."

"They call it *In Vitro Veritas*," Jake said. "If anything, *that's* what pisses everybody off."

"Huh?"

"*In Vitro Veritas*," Beth said dismissively. "It's a stupid wine pun." She turned to Spencer. "You can't really be serious about this whole demon thing."

"Sure, why not?"

"Why *not*? Have you even *watched* a horror movie?"

He gasped, looking almost ludicrously offended, and clapped an indignant hand to his chest like a pearl-clutching dowager.

"If you have," she went on, "you *know* what happens whenever a bunch of retards go fucking around with Ouija boards or old books in Latin or something."

"Yeah, but that's just *Paranormal Activity* bullshit," Spencer said.

She shook her head and raised her hands in the air. "Fine. Whatever. Download *Demon Summoning For Dummies*. Your funeral."

"Well, but," said Devon, "even if we really were going to—"

"What do you mean, well-but-even-if-really?" Jake interrupted. "It's a great idea!"

"It's a dumbfuck idea," Beth said.

"Even if it works?"

"*Especially* if it works."

"Which it won't," Devon said. "Right? Can't. Right? Nothing's going to happen."

She looked at him. "Have *you* even watched a horror movie?"

"Well, yeah, but..."

"Jeez, Bethany," Jake said. "Quit trying to talk us out of it."

"Like *I* could?" She scoffed. "Besides, somebody has to

shoot the video, *Jacob.*"

"Fuck, yeah!" said Spencer. "It'll be hilarious. Probably go fuckin' viral."

"But what if...what if something...does happen?" Devon asked.

"*Definitely* go viral," Beth said.

"Great." Marty hunched his shoulders.

"Internet sensation," Jake said. "We'll be famous!"

"If," Beth added with a sharp little glint in her eye, "you live."

"What?" Devon and Marty cast uneasy looks her way.

"Just saying," she said. "When stunts like this go wrong, they go way, *way* wrong. Some demon does show up and rip your faces off, I want to be there to say I told you so."

"Yeah, but if you're there, it'll rip your face off too," Jake said.

"Worth it to get the last word."

"But we'd be dead," said Devon. "What good's a video if we all end up dead?"

She flashed him a hard-edged, cynical grin. "Where do you think all those found-footage movies come from?"

"Perfect," Marty said. "From *Paranormal Activity* bullshit to *Blair Witch* bullshit."

"Don't forget *Weird Science* bullshit," Jake said. "Sexy Brit-babe in blue undies, a talking shit-pile, and *Iron Man* with a bra on his head."

Devon's expression proclaimed him utterly, utterly lost. Before anybody could begin to explain, they heard Brendan's car return, then Brendan himself thumping up the stairs. The apartment door swung open.

"Check *this* out," he proclaimed, beaming proudly.

It took the rest of them a few moments to recognize the oblong box he held up as a VHS tape in a cardstock sleeve. Serious old-school, a mere step removed from film-strip projectors and 8-track.

Marty took it and read the drippy-red clawstroke-font title aloud. "*Deadly Beauties IV: The Devil's Daughter.*"

"A horror movie?" asked Devon.

"A rare classic of the occult, vintage seventies."

"Rare classic of the occult?" Beth hoisted an eyebrow.

"Yeah, but does it have nudity?" asked Jake. "Priorities, bro."

"Boobs and bush everywhere, bro."

"Bush?" Devon echoed, askance.

Brendan bobbed his head. "That's what vintage seventies *means*. These ladies are *aaaaalll* natural."

Beth snatched the tape to study the cover: a terrified-looking man bound spread-eagle in a pentagram. Surrounding him were robed figures holding candles, the light of which cast a sexy shadow—hourglass figure, horns, tail, batwings—onto his chest hair and the treasure trail leading down his bare and oily midriff, where strategic scraps of cloth met bare-minimum decency standards over a bulge suggesting not all of him was as terrified as his expression seemed to claim.

"Nice tagline...*She'll Come When You Call*. Classy."

"Sounds like total crap," Marty said.

"*Vintage* total crap," Brendan said. "Vintage *seventies* total crap."

She turned the box over, skimming the text. "Varsity swim team on their way to a meet...wrong turn, bus breaks down...have to seek help in a strange, isolated village... beautiful women...sinister cult...insatiable appetites of a she-devil from Hell..."

"Sweet." Jake high-fived Brendan. "Where'd you get it?"

"My dad. He's got tons of this shit hidden in the garage. Movies, magazines. Bunches of church stuff, which is weird: naughty nuns, anal angels."

"He's religious?" Devon asked skeptically.

"No, that's the weird part. Or maybe the preggo-porn is the weird part; he's got a lot of that, too—"

"Dude!" cried Marty. "Sick!"

"Hey, all I know is, I first found his stash when I was ten, and I thought I died and went to titty heaven."

CHAPTER THREE
ANTICIPATION

Desire.

Desire and purpose.

Desire and hunger.

Hunger and purpose and need.

To crave and to serve.

To give and to take, to take and to give.

It is, it is, it is.

We are.

Many and one, one in many, one and many, many in one.

We are All. We are One.

Who will be? Which will be? Which shall become?

All and one and one and all.

Love and serve. Feed and need.

To urge and coax and taste.

To touch.

Kiss.

Lick.

Suck.

Taste and tease and take.

To engulf.

Draw deep, so deep.

To clasp moist-slick to slide and glide and milk yes milk the salt-milk the life-milk to pulse and squeeze.

So deep, so full, fill and fulfill.

Hunger and desire, hunger and need.

Need!

Need and purpose.

Our purpose.

We. One. All.

We serve. We crave.

Flesh oh flesh salt taste and tang.

The urge. The surge.

The urgency, surging, surging, grip and slip and slide-glide wet-tight to coax to milk, the milk, salt-life-milk and pump and flood, release.

To take.

And take.

And take some more.

More and more.

To feed. To drink. To suck and swallow, to engulf and encompass and absorb.

Take and take, the hunger, the need, the desire, the purpose.

Take and give. Give and give. Share and grow, grow many, grow strong.

Our purpose.

Which will be?

Which becomes?

We are All, All are One.

We crave. We serve.

One becomes.

And here, now, the Call.

INTERLUDE: VIGNETTES #1

You know how, in a lot of books, you get the obligatory info dump of town history, backstory, and character introduction? Yeah. This is one of those parts. This is where we'll take a quick overview of Fairmont and meet some of the people whose lives are about to be fucked over in the upcoming chapters.

A few of them may even deserve it. The dogfucker, for instance, and the eunuch. Others, the more innocent, the good and decent hard-working citizens, might not deserve it so much...but tough shit for them; evil doesn't play fairsies.

Onward!

***

Nestled in the picturesque wooded hills blah-de-blah natural beauty hiking day trips excursions et cetera et cetera charming inns bed-and-breakfasts cabins vacation rentals so on and so forth winery tours wine tastings art galleries quaint shopping district specialty foods fine eateries yadda-yadda perfect honeymoon locale or dream private getaway quiet scenic adult-oriented lay it on with a trowel.

Fairmont wasn't always like this.

Once, back in the day—the day being in the 1940s and 1950s—it was your typical example of classic Americana. White picket fences, ladies' bridge clubs, mens' bowling leagues, Veteran's Day parades, Fourth of July picnics, school concerts, speeches at the Shelter Park bandstand, bake sales, Community Civil Readiness drills.

Pleasantville bullshit, as Spencer might say.

Then came the decline, the beginnings of the struggle against slow, clawing attrition. The interstate went in, and what had once been a main highway became the road less traveled by. Stores closed. Families moved away. Soon, all that remained was yet one more downspiraling, dying town.

Until the vineyard craze hit. Until the area around Fairmont was discovered to be a sweet spot for grapes, as well as several varieties of apples, fruits, and berries. Enterprising developers glommed up the land, and before most of the locals knew what was happening, small privately-owned wineries were popping up everywhere.

Then came the revitalization, the renewal. A fancy downtown went in, packed with bistros and upscale shops and pedestrian strolling areas, and a surge of handcrafted this and artisinal that. Streets were given names like Merlot, Reisling, and Chablis—Rose-like-the-flower becomes Rosé-like-the-wine as it nears the nicer neighborhoods.

Today, tourists come and go. Some make annual events of it, particularly for anniversaries. Weddings are also big. There's a couple of time-share resorts, a gated RV community, a posh conference center for corporate retreats. No casino, of course, because that would be gauche.

It isn't exactly high on anybody's list of kid-friendly destinations, though. The businesses like it that way, not having to cater to noisy, grubby, demanding, picky little brats. None of the *good* restaurants have juvenile crap like chicken nuggets or hot dogs on the menu. A few don't even allow anybody under the age of thirteen. The nearest McPlayPlace is over in Winston City, the only day care is run by a creepy old lady and her creepier live-at-home nephew, and the toy stores are more aimed at well-to-do grandparents who'll spend way too much on gifts nobody wants.

But, most of all, the kid thing? That's important. That's the author pulling a deft bit of plot-prestidigitation on you, providing a plausible reason why there aren't a whole lot of children in town.

Because, see, this story's going to get all nasty with sex stuff, dubious issues of informed consent, nocturnal dream-demons and the like—it's a succubus book, here, people, what do you expect? And having a lot of younger characters around would just make everything a little *too* icky and weird. We have *some* standards, thank you very much!

***

So, about that dogfucker.

He was mentioned earlier, if only in passing. His name is Lewis, but he's known as Coach. He's been known as Coach since about the mid-1990s, and still is known as Coach, though he and Fairmont High parted ways some five years ago.

One too many instances of DUI they couldn't overlook, the school board says.

That dye-job biddy of a new lady principal having it in for him, Coach says.

Like Spencer, Coach is a Bodean, which may need further explanation.

Bodeans are your basic human barn cats: some friendly, some feral, none fully tamed.

Coach is—or was—one of the more semi-respectable members of the sprawling and probably-too-inbred clan. Under his guidance, the boys' basketball and girls' track teams in particular had several championship years. He saved up enough on a regular salary to buy himself a tidy rambler by the school instead of continuing to enjoy the more traditional shack-and-shantytown lifestyle of most of his kin.

He's still popular with the older teens and immature adults in town, because he'll buy them beer if they put up the cash. *Beer*, mind you. None of that whiny-winy shit for Coach Lewis Bodean. None of those microbrewsnob bottles, either. Real, proper, mass-produced American beer in real, proper, mass-produced aluminum cans. Many underage drinkers have earned their first head-pounding hangovers at Coach's place.

The downside to the arrangement, if it counts as a downside, is that hanging out at Coach's means listening to Coach dispense his sage advice and wise wisdom unto the brows and bosoms of the next generation. He may no longer be a member of the faculty, but as he sees it, he's still a teacher at heart.

In other words, they sit around and drink and listen to him lecture-gripe about women.

Coach has never been married. He has no kids of his own and damn well doesn't want them. He's seen more than enough train wrecks already, within his own extended tangle of relations, or passing through the hallowed halls of Fairmont High. Hell, you couldn't even turn on the television these days without witnessing nine miles of conniving bitchery.

And yet, hasn't it always been that way?

What a man has to go through to get laid…a million gauntlets to run and hoops to jump…and if she likes it too much, she'll turn clingy, start wanting commitments, go psycho if he tries to break things off…but if she regrets it later, she'll cry rape; even if he's found not guilty, forget it, there's a life as good as over. If *she'd* been boozed up, she's free-and-clear not accountable…but if *he'd* been, guess who's entirely to blame?

No one believes a man's story. It's always, *always*, his full-and-sole fault. Women had, in their scheming over thousands and thousands of years, seen to that, all right.

Likewise, the rubbers; for each who wouldn't go near a boner unless it was sealed in six layers of shrink-wrap—and never mind showering in a raincoat, diminishing a man's pleasure; never mind his opinion on the matter—there'd be another who might pin-jab it first or fish the used out of the trash, and bam, marriage-trap or a lifetime of child support.

Wasn't worth it, wasn't none of it worth it. Not in Coach Lewis Bodean's opinion.

Hence, the dogfucking.

Hence, his Roxie, his good ol' girl.

She's a big bloodhound-mix mutt, a clumsy-looking collection of long gangly legs, droopy jowls, floppy ears, and lolling slobbery tongue. Breath like the bottom of a dumpster in high summertime and paint-peeling farts.

A bitch, yes. A literal bitch to be sure. And she does have her wiles—the soulful eyes routine when he's having his dinner, by way of example. But the one bitch, the one female of any species, he can trust.

His Roxie, he knows, would never trick or betray him. All he had to do was keep her in kibble, give her a roof over her head and a yard to shit in. She'd never cry rape. She'd never make him wear a rubber, she was fixed anyway, and it sure wasn't as if he'd knock her up.

This, of course, is Coach's reasoning. As such reasoning goes, it isn't entirely un-sound.

We could look in on him late some night, after the beers had been drunk and the kids gone off to do whatever they did when they weren't receiving his sermons.

We could look in on him as he pats his mattress to beckon his good girl up onto the bed, as he slathers up his cock with Vaseline from the jumbo-size jar he keeps in the nightstand drawer, as he maneuvers her hind paws astraddle his hips and eases her haunches down so his grease-slicked cockhead pushes into the hot and fuming mess of her dogcunt.

We could watch as he fucks her in short, hard, fast thrusts…as she whines a little, confused like she always is, and stringers of drool splat on Coach's belly and chest…as his fists clench at coarse coat and loose skin…as he grunts and strains and spurts into her…as he collapses, spent, and tells her to go on and get down…as his limp cock slip-plops out of her like a stillborn puppy trailing a placenta of Vaseline and cum.

Yes, we could do that, we could look in on him and watch.

But it'd be sick, gratuitous, and wrong.

CHAPTER FOUR
LOCATION

A few days and several barrages of text messages back and forth later, Jake figured they were as ready as they were ever going to be.

He also figured, probably rightly, that if they waited too long or thought about it sober too much, it'd never happen. Someone would get cold feet and back out. Or Beth's sarcasm would turn to scorn and shame them to their senses. Or any of a number of possibilities.

Not that he really expected it to work...but what a kick in the head it'd be if it did! How cool would it be if they actually pulled it off?

Even if they didn't, it'd still be pretty damn awesome just to try. Better than another night of the same old sitting around playing video games. Something new. Something different. Exciting. An adventure.

When he told them where he wanted to make the attempt, he got some push-back and reluctance. But he wore them down, won them over. It wasn't as if they had many other options, and it was better to not get anybody else involved, anyway.

If it did work...

Which it won't, he could almost hear Beth saying in his head.

But if it *did*...

And hey, wasn't there a chance that it *might*?

More of a chance even than the rest of his friends knew, because he hadn't yet told them his personal special secret. He didn't want to say anything ahead of time, didn't want to have them give him a bunch of shit if nothing actually *did* happen—which, okay, it probably wouldn't—but on that off-chance, that slim and crazy off-chance...

So, after another round of texts to make sure they all knew the plan and would be there at the agreed-upon time, Jake gathered the printouts and his share of the ritual's supplies, and headed down the street to Shelter Park to start setting things up.

The name didn't, contrary to popular belief, come from the fact that a handful of homeless used it for an occasional campground. Jake's grandfather, a local history buff, had told him how that was where, once upon a time, everybody in town was supposed to go when the bombs flew. In a calm, cooperative, orderly fashion. There to wait out the nuclear firestorms, trust in their government, and be ready to emerge to reclaim and rebuild this most greatest of nations.

Or something like that. As if. Maybe once, maybe back then in the golden oldie days, but this was *today's* world. At the first sign of civilization collapse, it'd be road warriors, rape-gangs, and cannibalism in no time.

Most of the Fairmont wine-snob elite didn't even know about the old Community Civil Readiness program, let alone about the warren of bunkers, dormitories, tunnels, and storerooms honeycombing beneath the little half-ignored park.

Hell, most of the ordinary locals didn't know, either. Or didn't care anymore. Grade school kids heard about it as where high schoolers would to go to smoke and drink and make out; high schoolers forgot about it as soon as they found other places to go to smoke and drink and make out; junior high kids dared each other to venture down there as tests of bravery or rites of passage.

And there *were* the homeless. Not many, but a few. Drunks and crackheads and low-key crazies. As long as they didn't stray over to try panhandling in the tourist part of town so much that the rich people complained, the cops only made half-hearted efforts to move them along.

Two or three had their claims staked between the rear curve of the low amphitheater bleachers and the hedge—sleeping bags, shopping carts, an ancient army-green pup tent—but the bandstand steps and stage were deserted. So was the graffiti-covered cinderblock building that had once housed restrooms and a utility shed.

The shed's heavy double doors looked like they would screech and squeal rusty murder on their hinges, and slam shut with a huge echoing clatterbang that'd rip through the quiet darkness like a fart at a funeral. A stout bolt and looped length of padlocked chain secured their handles. As a finishing touch, some smartass had scrawled DONT DEAD OPEN INSIDE across them in black paint.

Jake just went around to the wedged-ajar door to the men's room, and into a chilly cave of chipped tiles, stained plaster, and windblown dry leaves. Though the fixtures had long since been removed, leaving capped pipes jutting from the floor where the stalls used to be, the facilities were still far from disused. His nose wrinkled at the ammoniac tang of pee both ancient and not-so, but it was a reflex and he barely noticed.

There was a big gaping crumbling-edged hole in one wall, with a hollow black space on the other side. He shined the light from his phone through it and saw the short drop— more than a step, less than a jump—onto the landing of a switchbacked flight of industrial metal stairs.

Down he went, treading on crushed cigarette butts and bits of broken glass. He tried to imagine the good citizens of Fairmont descending these steps in the calm and orderly fashion urged by those old pamphlets—women and children first, nobody panicking—and couldn't do it. Nope. It'd be pushing and shoving, trampling, screaming and chaos.

At the bottom, another door opened onto a hallway, perhaps originally done in that shade of hospital green somehow meant to be soothing. Wire-caged lightbulbs clung to the upper corners like weird spiders. Some of them even still worked, which was either impressive or unnerving, or maybe both. They shed a thin jaundice-yellow light, the color equivalent to the ammonia pee smell from above.

Helpful signs hung askew, labeling offices and cluttered storerooms, pointing directions to dormitories and mess halls. The furnishings—gunmetal grey desks, filing cabinets, swivel chairs—looked like they might've been kicked here all the way from 1948. Out-of-order drinking fountains, corroded fire extinguishers, and bulky prehistoric telephones stuck randomly from the walls like rock formations.

Surprising, really, Jake thought, that none of those urban spelunker types had sought it out yet. Or Fallout LARPers, if there was such a thing. He reminded himself to ask Marty. Marty would know. Marty wouldn't LARP himself, hell no, didn't go in for any of *that* brand of geek-shit (except collecting pictures of cosplay babes) but if it was a thing, he'd know.

Marty had even nicknamed the place for them: Vault 420. Partly because this was where they'd all sneak off to smoke before getting the apartment, and partly because the room they used most had a hubcap-sized clock on the wall with the hands perpetually frozen at guess-what-time. They'd considered it a favorable omen.

Opposite the perpetual 4:20 clock was a cheerful cartoon poster depicting cheerful cartoon people gathered at a dinner table: Mom serving a platter of meatloaf to Dad, Big Sis, and Little Bro, while a cheerful cartoon dog begged beside Little Bro's chair. REMEMBER, read the printed caption, FAMILY FIRST. To this, someone—presumably whichever smartass had also decorated the double doors topside—had added EAT YOUR.

Other than that, it was much the same as Jake remembered. An office of some sort at one time, with one of those big-ass metal desks and a filing cabinet tipped onto its side to serve as a bench, it still smelled of bygone weed. One of the miraculously still-working light fixtures was just outside, though sporadically sputtering and emitting a low, irritating, buzzing hum.

He set to shifting stuff about, clearing a wide space on the faded and discolored linoleum. In addition to the candles required for the ritual, he'd had the foresight to bring along a couple of little battery-powered clip lamps, arranging them so their bright cones spotlight the center of the floor.

Consulting the print-out pages from various demonology wikis, he went to work. By the time he heard the scuff and

38

thump and rustle of footsteps approaching, and familiar voices carrying strangely in the subterranean acoustics, he had the outline done and most of the glyphs and sigils chalked in.

"Wow, what a dump," Brendan said. "What a shit-hole."

"Yeah, well, you can leave any time," Beth replied.

"Hey, no, I'm not leaving, I was only saying."

"It is kind of…uh…run-down," said Devon, the new kid.

"'Course it is; they built it a hundred fuckin' years ago," Spencer said.

"Not a hundred," said Marty. "Maybe more like seventy."

They came in, pausing and looking impressed when they saw the progress Jake had already made. Even in the clip-lamp beams, the intricate pentacle with its rings of arcane symbols and designs was pretty cool; by candlelight, it would be spooky awesome.

Each of the other guys carried various bundles of what components they'd agreed to bring. Jake had told them it'd be more effective if everyone contributed something. So, Spence had some fresh-laid eggs from his Nana Nell's ratty-ass chicken farm…Devon brought a box of yeast-culture packets from his parents' bakery pantry as well as the glass windchime he'd volunteered…Brendan must've scoured several antique stores to find a brass bell and an old church censer…and Marty…

Marty grimaced as he presented a Shop-N-Go bag, into which was stuffed another Shop-N-Go bag and then another and another, like some kind of screwed-up nesting doll or baggie turducken. Inside all that plastic was a wad of convenience store restroom dispenser paper towels, and at the core of that was a slim brown paper bag. And, according to Marty, inside *that* was a wad of toilet paper, and inside *that*, the moon-blood of a nubile maiden.

"How did you even—" began Devon.

"You don't want to know," Marty said, shuddering.

"*I* want to know," said Beth.

"Yeah, me too," Spencer said.

"It was at work the other night, okay? This car pulls up

and a girl comes in, like in a real hurry, asks where we stock the, uh…the female products—"

"Tampons," Beth said in a clear, loud voice.

He flinched. "Yeah, those."

"You've gotta get over that squeamish thing if you're ever gonna get a girlfriend," Jake said, placing silver plates at the points of the pentacle. He'd 'borrowed' them from the fancy restaurant in the clubhouse of Vintner's Green, the golf course where he worked. "She might expect you to do real-life grownup stuff like pick 'em up at the store for her."

"My mom asked me and my dad to do that once," Devon said. "There were like a million kinds. He had to ask some lady for help."

Beth heaved a sigh and shook her head.

"So, she grabs a box and books it to the bathroom," Marty said. "Then she comes back out, apologizes the whole time she's paying, says it was an emergency, she thought she had some but they must've been in her other purse…she wouldn't shut *up*... it was a nightmare."

"And then, what?" asked Spencer. "After she's gone, you duck into the ladies' room and fish the dead mousie out of the trash?"

"Dead…?" began Devon.

Spence mimed holding up something as if dangling from a tail, or a string, and Devon turned greenish.

"That is so wrong," Beth said. "Not to mention fucking creepy and probably illegal."

Marty nodded miserably. "I know, and sick, and disgusting…I almost puked."

"But," Brendan said, "important part: was she a nubile maiden?"

"What do you want from me, dude? She was a girl! I dunno! A chick, a hottie, high school, maybe college…I dunno! Am I supposed to quiz her about her noob-ility?"

"Chill, Mart-O," Spencer said. "You did good. 'Specially for a total wussy-pussy, you did good."

"Yeah, great, thanks, whatever. Can we just do this already?"

"We got everything?" Brendan asked Jake. "We set?"

"Almost. I still need to do the salt and twine, then we light the candles. Beth, how's it look?"

She boosted herself up to sit on the battered old desk, heels of her equally battered old Converse high-tops bumping atonal clonks, and leaned back so she could frame the whole scene with her phone. "Ready to film the FAIL. Viral video internet sensation, here we go."

"Ha, ha. Okay, Spence, shut the door."

"We're shutting the door?" Devon asked.

"You want anybody walking in on this?"

"Well, no, but..."

"It'll be fine," Beth said. "As long as nobody farts."

"Now you tell us," said Spencer, moving to the door. "Guess we shouldn't'a scarfed all those fuckin' Shop-N-Go burritos on the way over."

Jake finished tracing the chalk lines with runnels of salt, spilling them from a curled fist like one of those monk-types making a mandala out of colored sands. He began winding the black yarn around the waxy bases of the white candles— also 'borrowed' from Nineteen On The Green. "Okay, Brendan, Dev, be ready with the bell and the chime for when I start lighting these up—"

"*Definitely* no one fart," Beth said.

"We are all gonna die," Marty said. "That's it, game over, we are all gonna die."

CHAPTER FIVE
INCANTATION

Found footage.

Beth held her phone steady, shifting her gaze back and forth from the screen to the scene.

As if the world needed more video evidence of guys being stupid horndogs. Or more video evidence of a bunch of retards trying to fuck around with the occult. Fuck around but literally, in this case.

Typical.

She kind of wished something *would* happen. Just to see the looks on their faces. Just to watch them shriek like little girls, wet their pants, freak out, and run. Like those compilation clips of oh-so-tough dudebros going through a jump-scare haunted house or getting epicly pranked with a fake snake or some shit.

To give Jake credit, he'd done a decent job organizing them and setting the stage. The diagram he'd copied from whichever demonology website was complex and intricate, not just a plain old goth/metalhead pentagram. The smaller designs etched within its outer ring looked suitably astrological, alien, Lovecraftian, and weird all in one. A couple of them, she had to admit, were downright disturbing in an unsettling way she couldn't quite put her finger on. She didn't remember having seen them on his various printed-out pages and reminded herself to ask him about them later.

Later, when they'd stopped laughing about their failure and what asses they'd made of themselves.

With the clip-lamps off, and the five candles lit— Brendan ringing the brass bell and Devon tinking plinks from his mom's glass wind chime as Jake touched a match to each wick, counting them off in halting Latin—the grubby confines of Vault 420 took on a shifting, shadowy,

42

moody atmosphere. The flames glimmered in the basin of pure water, even if the water was a jug of distilled they'd picked up at the Winston City Wal-Mart and the basin a huge gnawed-on plastic dog dish Spence had gotten from Coach's garage, Coach's dog Roxie having been upgraded to sturdy stainless steel.

Once they'd all quit wisecracking and snickering, hushed up and acted more serious, it almost started to seem halfway legit. Each of the guys had taken their places at one of the points of the pentacle, like in that hilariously bad *Devil's Daughter* movie they'd watched. All they needed was the hooded robes.

Okay, no, they'd need more than the hooded robes. Positioned like dutiful little cultists or not, they were still a far sight from even the 'vintage seventies' idea of devil-worshipers, which evidently really *had* involved a lot of boobs and bush, as well as slender young studs with porn-staches and body hair, like contestants in a Freddie Mercury look-alike contest.

She glanced from Spencer to Marty, from Devon to Brendan, to Jake.

Talk about a far-fucking-cry…

Jake swung the censer in precise looping arcs. Scented smoke puffed from it in drifting spirals, twining around the tendrils rising from the candles. Much different types of smoke than they were used to, adding to the general eeriness of the ambiance. For a second or two, her eyes even played hypnotic tricks, suggesting the fine greyish wisps formed fleeting shapes…letters…symbols.

Yeah, and animators really *did* put subliminal sex messages into Disney cartoons.

The guys had fallen silent, even Spencer, as Jake waved the censer around, reciting more words in halting Latin. It was, Beth reflected, still an improvement on his mangled attempts in Ms. Gateaux's French class. Not that many of her students had been there out of a love of language; it was a graduation requirement, and given the choice between a hot lesbian or the hundred-year-old gimp who taught Spanish, well…

There was a pause, nobody moving, nobody speaking.

The smoke hung. The candleflames had stopped flickering, and burned standing straight and tall in the motionless air.

Beth noticed they all—even she—had fallen into a slow pattern of breathing in unison. How was that for creepy? This was how people psyched themselves right the fuck out, or right the fuck into believing this shit.

Her mind suddenly spat up memories of a much-younger Beth, a Bethie who slept over at a birthday party for her older cousins and they played light-as-a-feather, they played Mary-in-the-Mirror, they would have been all over that Charlie-Charlie game if it'd been big back then.

That little Beth…who wasn't yet ready to rule out either Santa Claus or the boogeyman…the Bethie still several years from coming home to find her brother, hanging from the banister in their entryway, purple and gurgling…

That Beth had been, in those moments, utterly convinced.

Her mind also spat up her own voice: Have you even *watched* a horror movie?

"Offer the hen's egg, freshly laid," Jake said.

He no longer sounded halting, jokey, or unsure. He sounded…charismatic, even a little bit…sexy.

A clammy shiver slithered down her spine. Talk about unsettling.

Spencer leaned forward, holding one of the brownish eggs in both hands. He cracked the shell on the brim of the plastic dog dish and emptied its gloopy contents into the water. The yolk, swimmy in its puddle of clear gelatinous whites, made an irregular, yellow, lidless eye.

"Offer the moon-blood of a nubile maiden," Jake said.

Marty, with more grimaces and flinches, unwrapped the layers of his gross-gotten bundle until he reached the wad of stain-splotched toilet tissue with a straggle of string trailing from one end. He flicked it into the basin, then scrubbed his hand furiously on his pants, making thick trying-not-to-hork noises.

The tissue paper bloated out and blossomed like a weird

fungal flower, its maroon crustings rehydrating to red, as it absorbed and went soggy. Some caught on the egg-edges and drew down jellyfish streamers with it as it sank.

"Offer the lock of virgin's hair," Jake said next.

This, obviously, had been a source of contention; no way in hell any of them were going to own up, no matter how painfully evident might be the truth. In the end, to let everybody save face, Brendan raided the combs of his younger brothers.

"They're twelve," he'd explained, "nerdy as hell, and Village-of-the-Damned creepy-looking. Be a miracle if they ever get to first base with a girl."

He opened a zip-top bag and shook several thin white-blond strands onto the surface of the now-murkier water.

The candle flames continued not to waver. In fact, though she couldn't be sure it wasn't just her eyes, she could've sworn they all burned at exactly the same height, color, and shape.

Suggestibility sure was one devious, insidious bastard.

"Offer the sacrifice of innocent life," Jake said.

And by now, damn it, he didn't just *sound* charismatic and sexy, he was *looking* it, too. His normal clean-cut and wholesome boy-band/pretty-boy/boy-next-door look, which made him perfect for his job as a golf caddy for rich tourists, had somehow taken on a wickedness...

It was an effect of the candles, the lighting, the smoke.

Had to be.

Devon tore open the packet of yeast cultures from his parents' bakery pantry and sprinkled out a fine rain of gritty, grainy powder. His brace-yourself expression simultaneously proclaimed ludicrousness and guilt. They were *yeasts*, for fuck's sake, not even brine shrimp or crickets. It wasn't as if billions of them didn't go into bread every day...you want genocide, you want ovens...

Beth shook herself. Was she honestly sitting here, filming this, equating a packet of goddamn baker's yeast to the Holocaust?

There were no flashes or sparks or *Horton-Hears-A-*

Who-esque choruses of tiny doomed screams. Just that gritty rain of particles, some of which clumped and some of which spread, and the contents of the basin grew murkier still.

Jake undid his jeans.

The spell of intent silence was abruptly broken.

"Dude! What the hell?" Marty yelped.

"Don't tell me you forgot what else it calls for," said Jake. "The new-spilled seed of a virile youth."

"Yeah, but..." Even Brendan looked askance. "You're gonna just...whip it on out right here in front of everybody?"

"Hey, whoa," Beth said, tipping her phone toward the floor. "There goes our PG-13 rating."

Candles sputtered. Light danced and shadows leaped. The smoke whirled and whorled in slow, lazy hazes.

"So don't watch," Spencer said. "Nobody says you gotta watch."

"Are *you* gonna watch?" Devon asked.

"No fuckin' way." He barked a laugh. "I wanna look at a dick, I got one of my own."

"Watch, or don't, *I* don't care," Jake said. "But we need to complete the ritual. No sense stopping now."

"Fine," Beth said, letting the edge of a challenging sneer sharpen her tone. "You want me to film it?"

"Your call." He didn't wink, didn't so much as glance at her, only unzipped the rest of the way.

"Dude," Marty said again, in a weak, protesting bleat.

It was like a roomful of kids trying not to be called on by the teacher. Beth kept her phone on record but aimed anywhere besides Jake...capturing the uncomfortable reactions of the others...capturing the noises, the sliding of skin on skin, the ragged changes in breathing...

Had it gotten weirdly warm and steamy in this closed, crowded room?

Had it gotten intensely awkward and more than a little personal?

...a muffled low groan as if through clenched teeth...

Damn it, was she blushing?

Was anybody else?

46

Who knew?

Nobody could look at anybody.

...a liquid splatter and splash...

...Jake's husky exhalation like a sigh...

...his utterance of something in a language she couldn't name, and a voice even more strikingly unlike his own...

...there was silence again, but for the rush-thump of her own pulse way too quick in her ears...

...then the rustle and zip, presumably signaling that the danger zone was now passed.

She checked via her phone first, as if the avoidance of direct eye contact would somehow make a difference—like dealing with goddamn Medusa—and once assured it was safe, shot Jake her best withering annoyed glare. He either missed it completely or really *didn't* care; his attention was fixed on the basin at the center of the pentagram.

Which now had, in addition to its already nasty stew of contents, Jake's fresh contribution. Points for marksmanship; he seemed to have pretty well hit the target. Kind of a miracle, from what Beth understood of guys and their squirtguns—

Her thoughts got no further, derailing in a jumble of shock.

The basin.

The pentagram.

All the trash-talk they'd done, all the smirking and joking, about how wild it'd be if something actually happened...

Never believing it. Never expecting it. Not for one second thinking any of it could be real.

Knowing the whole thing was safe, secure, harmless, and stupid.

But, then, holy shit.

Holy fuck.

Something happened.

Something actually *happened.*

CHAPTER SIX
REACTION

The candles burned a sudden bright clear blue-green like hissing jets of gasflame.

The lines of salt ignited, tracing the symbols and sigils in racing gunpowder fireworks sparks.

Everyone squeaked or shouted something or another—wordless outcries, exclamations, shocked obscenities.

"Holy *shit!*"

"What the *fuck?*"

"Did you *see*—?"

"How the *hell*—?"

Devon felt his heart lurch like it wanted to shoot straight up through the top of his head. Beth jerked, heels clonking again on the side of the desk. Spencer recoiled so fast he might've given himself whiplash.

Then, there was a general spate of weak, shaky, embarrassed laughter.

"Jesus, dude!" Marty wheezed and thumped a fist on his chest. "Almost pissed myself!"

"Ha, good one," said Brendan, with an unconvincing attempt at nonchalance. "Nice trick, bro. You got us."

"*Not* funny," Spencer said. "Sincerely, not fuckin' funny at all."

"How did you do that?" Beth demanded of Jake. "Pyrotechnics? Chemicals in the candles and salt?"

Jake didn't reply. He stared with wide eyes at the basin, where a thick bubble had formed on the cloudy, congealed surface.

"And, what, you put something under the dog-dish?" asked Marty. "A heating element or something?"

"Uh, eew," Devon said. "Enough, huh?"

The bubble bulged. It swelled. It grew.

Trembling, pent-up, eruptive. Like a big watery blister, a zit ready to pop.

"If that slop bursts all over us..." Brendan said.

"Yeah, no shit," Spencer said. "Jake, knock it the fuck off."

Jake still didn't reply, still only stared. His eyes were huge. His face was ashen, weird in the blue-green underlighting of the intense, hissing gasflame candles.

"Jake?" Beth asked, sounding half-annoyed but half-worried as she slid off the desk.

If he was putting them on, it was an Oscar-caliber performance.

The bulbous, quavering, growing bubble resembled something from one of those thermal mudpuddles at Yellowstone. Sulfurous hot springs and simmering cauldrons of toxic sludge. Splurting and blorping in a flatulent cacophony of rotten-egg stench.

And there was a whiff of that, too, wasn't there? More than a whiff, mixed with other pungent, unpleasant smells. Sourdough starter, yeasty and teeming. The spunk-funk of cum and wank-sweat. A heavy and dark kind of blood-stink, girl-stink, secretive, cursed.

Much more than a whiff.

A downright reek.

"Gah, phew!" Marty cried, waving a hand in front of his face.

Getting stronger. Lingering in the air, warm and moist, musky, a permeating miasma.

"What *is* that?"

"*Whoa* it's foul!"

As the bubble got bigger. And bigger. An inflating, expanding, festering pustule.

"Guys..." Devon said.

"Knock it off!" repeated Spencer. "It wasn't fuckin' funny to start with, and—"

"It's for real," Jake said, in a slow, sleep-dreamy tone.

"Oh bull-fuckin'-shit—"

"No, really, it is." He blinked at them. He grinned. "It's working. We did it."

"Guyyyyys..." Devon said again, drawing the word out into a nervous whine.

The bubble had mushroomed far beyond the basin's capacity, rising like a grotesque misshapen souffle. Or something hideously birthed from one of those As-Seen-On-TV egg-cookers, extruding in a spongy mass.

And the *smell*! A gagging, gorge-heaving *smell* they could practically *taste*, could practically *feel*, like a scum, like a film on their skins!

"Oh dude it stinks!" Marty urped and clapped a hand over his mouth.

"Don't you hurl, don't you damn dare," Beth told him.

Bloated. Overripe. Gelatinous and slick with milky skeins, with ropy-wet reddish veins. An immense pregnant belly, straining, way past term. An udder, curdled and spoiled, about to explode from within. Shiny, infected boils needing lancing. Painful pus-filled pimples. Brimming, seething, volcanic.

"She's gonna blow," Spencer said, with a sick note of fascination.

"Better not; this is a new goddamn shirt!" Brendan said.

"Stop it, Jake!" Devon pleaded.

"I can't."

Beth got in his face. "Quit screwing around!"

"I'm not!"

"Well then who the hell *is*?"

Before he could answer, if he was going to answer, if he could answer at all, the bubble burst in a rupturing, horrible, noisome, squelching geyser.

Doing a six-part harmony wail of disgust, they all flung their arms over their heads, trying to shield themselves. They spun, or ducked, or hunched in on their shoulders like desperate turtles.

Oh, and the smell, the stench, the godawful *reek*—!

But nothing touched them.

Devon, peeking against his will and very much against his good judgment through the crook of a bent elbow, saw the gobbets and gouts of semi-coagulated fluid spew and roil as if channeled, as if confined in some sort of invisible lava-lamp chimney, some sort of glass-walled and weirdly angular cylinder...

The pentagram.

Where the salt outlines glowed like eerie crystalline embers, and the lengths of black yarn strung between the blue-burning candles looked spun from white fire.

The glop from the bubble struck the inside of that unseen barrier with a gooshy patter of squishes and trickles and spongy clots, and began sliding downward in coursing rivulets and slimy snail-trails.

It was, he thought, like seeing slushy rain or fresh bug guts on a windshield. Or when someone hocked a fat wet loogie on the other side of a windowpane. Or watching one of those sticky-gummy toy octopus things roll and slither-ooze its way down a wall or a mirror.

More had struck Vault 420's ceiling and showered back onto the floor in plops and drips and dribbles, but still only within the confines of the pentagram. Some landed on the underside of the basin, the big chewed plastic dog-dish having flipped entirely over at the force of...of whatever had just happened.

He very gingerly lowered his arms. He risked breathing—when had he held his breath? he had no clue—and found that the godawful reek wasn't so godawful after all. The worst of the stench had passed somehow, and what remained was much more bearable.

Not even unpleasant. Almost familiar.

Sourdough starter, he'd thought a moment ago. Nasty on its own, when it was a foaming and fermenting lump in a jar...but, as it transformed...it became...something else...

"Whuh—" rasped Spencer in a dusty croak. He coughed, licked his lips with a dry, lizardy sound, cleared his throat as if it hurt to do so, and tried again. "*What* the fuckin' *fuck?*"

"No kidding," Beth said.

Hesitantly, the others lowered their arms, raised their heads, and looked around at each other. Mouths worked, but nobody seemed to have anything else coherent to say.

Whoosh, and darkness.

The unnatural blue-green flames of the candles snuffed out. The sparkler-glittering salt crystal embers and white-fire yarn extinguished.

All six of them cried out again, brief shrieks followed by cussing.

Crazy, streaky, after-images sketched negative-color spiderwebs across Devon's vision. The only other light source was the dimness of Beth's phone, until Marty and Brendan, blundering around, managed to click on the clip-lamps in twin harsh brilliant bright cones.

"Okay," Marty said, like someone trying to muster his dignity. "How many of you jerks were in on that?"

Spencer rounded on him. "The fuck do you mean, in on it?"

"Sure you weren't; this whole thing was your idea!"

"Bite me! It was Jake's brilliant-ass plan!"

Brendan jabbed an accusing thumb at Beth. "Yeah, and *hers* to video the whole thing, make us look like morons! Internet sensation, my balls!"

"Oh right," she shot back, "and *you* just *happened* to find your dad's dirty devil movies!"

"*I* didn't punk anybody!"

"Me neither!" Devon said.

And boom, they was arguing, protesting and denying and flinging wilder and wilder accusations.

Except for Jake, who just stood there. Didn't bust a gut that they'd fallen for his prank, didn't try to defend himself, didn't admit it, didn't anything. Just stood there. Looking at the design he'd drawn on the shabby room's cheap linoleum floor.

Devon followed his gaze. The first thing he noticed was that the candles, once clean white pillars, were now just lumpy blobs the color of old, rancid lard. The lines of salt, also once clean and white, looked like the ashes left over after those Fourth of July snake pellets. Only little charred twists remained of the black yarn.

The design itself, once precise, was a scuffed, scattered

mess. Of the basin's former contents, most of the spillage had already dried to a brittle crack-glaze, and the bigger clots resembled runny, discolored, underdone dumplings.

"Hey," Jake said. "Would everybody shut up for a second?"

Several angry pairs of eyes turned his way. If he was about to apologize, the sullen sets of their jaws declared, it had better be pretty damn good.

"We might have a problem."

"Bet your ass we do," Spencer said. "I want to know which of you—"

"We *all* did, okay? We were all in on it together, and it worked."

"Jake, Jesus—" Beth said.

"How dumb do you think we are?" Brendan asked.

"No, seriously, I mean it. You saw the flames change color—"

"Yeah, from your rigged candles," said Marty. "And we smelled whatever you put in the bowl!"

"I didn't rig anything. We conducted a real ritual."

"The fuck we did!" Spencer swept his arm in an arc. "You see any sexy naked demon chicks here?"

Beth set her fists on her hips. "Or is that the problem? You think you summoned the wrong thing? Okay. What, then? Where is it? What's the big deal?"

He pointed at the dog-dish, which sat upside-down in the now-ruined pentagram.

It moved. It rose and fell, and twitched, as if something was alive underneath.

The others shook their heads, rolled their eyes, made exasperated noises, muttered stuff like "oh for fuck's sake" and "dude, c'mon, let it go" and "enough already, okay?" and "you are *such* an asshole!"

Brendan, throwing Jake a contemptuous look, kicked apart more of the salt-ash lines, bent over, and grabbed the gnaw-marked plastic.

"What are you doing?" Jake reached to stop him but Brendan jerked away.

"Getting it over with so we can go home," he sneered. "It'll be a fake spider or a rubber hand, oh ooh eek scary—"

Whatever was under there shot out so fast as soon as he lifted the edge that they all jumped, then burst out laughing because it was so obviously some stupid prank joke after all, some wind-up toy or RC car modded to look like a weird gross slug monster with turquoise-glowstick waggling feelers and wrinkled folds of loose slimy skin and knobbly clusters of grapelike growths.

Only, it wasn't.

Wasn't a toy, wasn't a prop, wasn't CGI.

And it went straight for Brendan.

INTERLUDE: VIGNETTES #2

That was a rotten place to leave things hanging. Don't you hate it when bastardly writers pull such manipulative tricks?

What did it say in those Community Civil Readiness pamphlets? Oh yes, to proceed in a calm and orderly fashion. Which is, I'm sure, just what the guys will do. They'll approach this surprising development with mature, appropriate, level-headed...

Ah, balls, you don't believe that any more than I do.

They'll totally panic and flip their shit.

It'll be great.

Well, not for them. Especially not Brendan, who made the dumbest of all dumbass mistakes. Characters never do learn. You see it every time. They say stuff like "there's no way anyone could have survived such a (fall/fire/fill-in-the-blank)," or they tentatively creep nearer the maniacal killer's sprawled and motionless body, or they tell themselves something couldn't possibly be for real.

And when that snaps back to bite them on the ass, don't we all kind of feel, as the song says, they had it comin'?

The hapless dopes with no clue anything weird's going on, though...the regular people just out there leading their lives...

Sucks to be them, my friend. Sucks to be them.

***

There are, of course, the Fairmont elite, as have already been touched upon. The winery crowd—Troy-fucking-Cahill of Cahill Cellars and his family, the Farcastles, the Vandivers, the silver-fox gay couple who own *Le Prestige du Vin*, others. And the hotel crowd—Sebastian Abbott, Cynthia-Lynne's

55

uncle, chief among them. You'd think he modeled his life after that oily bastard Ben Horne from *Twin Peaks*.

They may—in fact, forget *may*, they certainly *do*—look down their noses and sneer at the likes of the Bodeans. *Those* people, they say. As if they, on their lofty mountains, are above and removed from any whiff of shame or scandal.

Yeah, right. They're just as bad. In some ways, they're worse.

Addiction is addiction, whether it's home-labbed meth from a rust-raddled backwoods trailer or the first-class imported stuff. Abuse is abuse, whether it's trailer-trash whaling on their sassbacking snotnoses in the Winston City Wal-Mart or Vivian Farcastle grinding out lit cigarettes on the wizened flesh of her bedridden father-in-law and blaming their Cambodian housekeeper.

***

But, instead of the rich wine-snobs, let's consider some of the ordinary citizens of Fairmont, who neither suspect nor deserve the crazy infernal shitstorm about to descend on their lives. When those lives have already not been untouched by various tragedies, difficulties, and losses.

***

Let's start with Beth's mom, Suzette.

She's a stylist at Belle Salon. And, yes, whenever Beth tells anyone that, Beth with her spiky hair and grungy clothes and eyebrow piercings, she gets a Look: *Your* mom? A *beautician*? *Your* mom?

Yet, there it is. Belle Salon is a nice one, too, catering to the tourist ladies who leave better tips. Which is important, because Suzette is a widow, a single mom without many other options.

Her husband died—brain aneurysm, no warning, just pop and thump down he went—when Andrew was three and Suzette six months pregnant with Beth. He'd been an artist, a freelance illustrator, which had been great for looking after the house and the toddler, but not so great in terms of, oh, say, income or insurance.

His family, button-down professionals to a one, blamed Suzette for encouraging him to chase his dreams and wanted nothing further to do with her or the children. *Her* family, particularly her over-involved mother and busybody sisters, would have been only too happy to help...on their terms.

So, there was Suzette, left trying to raise two small kids pretty much on her own, putting them first, struggling to make ends meet and provide them a loving home.

You might think, well, no wonder Beth turned out the way she did. But Beth, for all of her surliness and attitude, kicks in most of her meager lock-shop paycheck to help with bills, despite Suzette's wish she save up for college.

It's Andrew who's the problem, sort of. Andrew, who never got over being alone in the house all day with his dead daddy. Andrew, who always had trouble in school, who needed counseling they couldn't afford, whose first and only girlfriend dumped him for his first and only best friend.

He hanged himself. Beth, then in junior high, found him. She saved him. Cut him down, did rescue breathing, kept him alive until the ambulance arrived.

Beth herself, in the darker parts of her mind, wishes she hadn't ditched her afternoon classes that day. Wishes she hadn't been so quick and decisive when she opened the door and saw her brother's dangling, twitching feet. Wishes she hadn't had a jackknife in her pocket, or she hadn't paid attention the day they learned about CPR.

She wonders if her mother has similar thoughts.

The horrible truth is that, sometimes, Suzette *does*.

Andrew isn't Andrew anymore. Andrew is a lump, a meatsack, a strange vacant-eyed beanbag of flesh. Almost a vegetable...except, vegetables don't have random fits of wailing and groaning and flinging aimless arms around.

They couldn't take care of him, not at home, and even applying for assistance wouldn't cover the costs of a full-time nurse. They had to send him away. To one of those places, those state-run grim places.

Suzette visits when she can, but gas prices are high and the car needs a new everything, and bus tickets and motel rooms are way beyond her budget, and her debts are like the big rock that guy in the story has to forever push up a hill.

The ladies at the salon—customers as well as her fellow beauticians—often encourage her to take some time for herself. To get out. To go out, go shopping, go dancing, go to bars and movies, meet men. She's still a young woman, they tell her, young enough, attractive. It's never too late to start over, to try again. Why, she has the whole rest of her life ahead of her!

The very idea makes Suzette want to simultaneously laugh and cry.

***

And what about Devon's parents, Maggie and Dan? We haven't heard much about them, beyond their plans to make a go of their little bakery/bistro in town.

Which has been a fuckton of work, let me tell you. Opening your own business means long damn hours, no sick days, hassles with loans and inspections, delays, budgets, exhaustion, and toil. Most of them fail within the first year anyway. You'd have to be crazy to try it. Crazy, dedicated, and willing to bust your ass.

They met in culinary school, Dan having washed out of basic training on account of a hitherto unknown heart murmur, Maggie wanting to follow in *her* mom's pastry-chef footsteps. Neither were superstars. They busted their asses as required, took whatever jobs they could find, two or three at a time, double shifts, triple. They scrimped and saved, lived in cramped studios, used food banks, shopped thrift stores.

Always with their eyes on the prize. Someday. Some day.

They're also a mixed-race couple, which shouldn't matter in this day and age.

A baby was *not* part of the initial plan. Not then. Not for years, not until they were established, had their own place up and running and successful enough to support them.

It was a tough call. They agonized, but ultimately decided to make the best of it somehow. And, a good thing they did…six years later, Maggie got diagnosed with ovarian and uterine cancer.

Devon doesn't know. Not about how close of a coin-flip his own life was, and not the details of his mom's surgery. He remembers visiting her in the hospital, bringing her flowers. He remembers being her special helper at home in the weeks afterward, feeling proud of himself when he could bring her a cup of tea or her medicine or a book while she rested. He remembers his dad being confident and brave.

He doesn't remember how wan-looking she was, how hollow-eyed, how often she cried. He doesn't remember, once, getting up in the middle of the night for a drink of water and finding Dad sitting at the kitchen table in the dark with his face in his hands and his shoulders shaking and a mostly-empty bottle of whiskey at his elbow.

It's never occurred to him to ask, or even wonder, why he's an only child. That's just how it is. Shrug. How it's always been.

CHAPTER SEVEN
CONFUSION

It wasn't a stampede at first, Beth would think later. Stampedes involved stupid, panicked animals running the same direction in a frenzied herd

They had the stupid, the panicked, and the frenzied parts down.

But same direction was like One Direction...fuck *that* noise!

Unlike terror-stricken cattle or bargain-mad Black Friday Doorbuster shoppers, there in Vault 420, the six of them ran in *every* direction, *all* directions, more than seemed humanly possible.

Given what they were trying to get away from, more than humanly possible right then seemed perfectly reasonable.

It squelch-lunged toward Brendan faster than fast.

The sounds it made as it moved were worse than the smell, and the sight of it worse than the sound, and the brain-hurting horrible hideous *unreality* of it was worst of all, worse than anything...except the prospect of its *touch*.

How it might *feel*—way, *way* worse than it looked, sounded, or smelled!

The very idea was exponentially more mind-twistingly horrifying.

Fast. So fast. Faster than fast.

Squelch-lunging toward Brendan.

The size of, and resembling, a cross between a half-deflated football—go, Patriots!—and one of those fuck-ugly Shar-pei pug dogs...but not a dog, not a football...naked mole rats, giant raisins, blobfish...subterranean and deep-sea glowing things...bug larva, gloopy handfuls of fish roe and frog eggs, microscope freakshow magnified a thousand times...

Nope.

Something gave way in her head. Sanity abdicating. A fuse blew, a switch flipped, something visceral and atavistic and primal and raw triggered every synapse and nerve ending with the same flashing neon klaxon message.

ALL THE FUCKING NOPE.

It went for Brendan, luminescent feelers waggling, the wrinkled folds along its loose, wobbly, flabby body parting with moist slurp-smacking noises.

Revealing orifices within. Slippery, glistening orifices. Orifices lined with fleshy sea-anemone polyps that undulated, flexed, extruded, retracted. White-tipped, then pinkish, shading to crimson and a deep throbbing purple.

As gag-worthy as the initial stink of it had been, once it smooched open those wet, gaping, sloppy, labial apertures—

Because what wafted from them, warm and steamy, were scents almost enticing. Evocative. Intriguing. Scents of baking bread, simmering gravy, tropical flowers, meat pies, perfume, hot fresh buttered popcorn, bacon, and sex.

Not a stampede.

A crazy fucking mosh-pit melee free-for-all.

Slamming into each other, into furniture, into walls. Tripping over all the random shit they'd left on the floor. Stepping on candles that rolled like skates beneath their feet. Into puddles of wax like cartoon banana peels. Falling. Scrambling. Screaming. Pushing and pulling and flailing.

Someone kicked the dog-dish and it flipped like a tooth-marked tiddlywink, pinwheeling more droplets of noxious slime. The stalled 4:20 clock got knocked down, clobbered Spencer, damn near flattened him—they built them heavy in those days, solid, industrial. The sheaf of printed-out papers were footprint-squished into the sludge and salty ashes. Marty tangled himself up in the Shop-N-Go bags and went into a thrashing epileptic seizure-dance. One clip-lamp shined askew at the ceiling. The second swung around in a crazy spotlight.

Jake and Devon were each trying to push the other one out of the way as Beth elbowed between them; all three went over in a jumble of limbs. A head mashed into her boobs and she didn't know whose and didn't care because her palm slid-skidded on the floor and for the most fleeting but awful instant of her life, she felt a mucoid slithering squirm under her hand and—

ALL THE FUCKING NOPE!!!

Brendan, on the floor, howling and shrieking.

It was on him.

It was *on* him!

Quavering. Pulsating. Rippling.

She thought of partly-filled water balloons and partly-drained waterbeds and understuffed beanbag chairs and those weird water-wigglie toys like supple alien dildos, and *that* reminded her of some nasty gelatin-egg thing on the internet and glorpy *Futurama* brain slugs and leeches and jellyfish and—

NOPE NOPE NOPE NOPE!!!

Then Spencer, reeling and staggering, incoherently bawling his entire repertoire of filthy words, blundered against the door and somehow fumbled it open.

The sputtering jaundice-yellow light from the ancient still-working fixture was a glorious golden beacon, a heavenly-choir radiant salvation, as if the strains of *Ode To Joy* cascaded in an angelic crescendo.

And *then* it was a stampede, a chaotic but purposeful surge, Black Friday Doorbusters let us the fuck *out* of here, charging and bottlenecking, logjamming in the doorway, fighting their way through in a crazy-blind mob.

Out.

Out into the hall. Out and fucking *away*, which way any way didn't matter just *move your ass **GO!***

Just go, go, go.

No stopping no looking back no nothing only *run*.

Coach, had he still been coaching, would've been impressed. His winning track and field teams couldn't have made better time in whatever sort of clusterfuck obstacle course it became. Sprints and hurdles and relay-race, not so much a handing off of batons as slapping, goading, and shoves.

Stairwell. Stairs. Pounding up them, and if her foot caught under the metal lip of a step she'd be lucky to only shatter her chin lose some teeth bite off her tongue break her nose gash her face open split ear to ear like the fucking Joker why so serious and maybe to be *really* lucky she'd snap her damn neck crack her skull open and die because dying might be preferable to having to deal with…deal with what…deal with that…what she'd seen what that *was* what they'd done!

The stairs, up and up, to the top, through the hole in the wall, the pee-smelling chilly tile of the long-abandoned men's room and the echoing madhouse clamor of their voices.

Screaming and swearing and wailing and laughing the loon-laughs of lunatics gone completely bugshit around the bend.

CHAPTER EIGHT
RATIONALIZATION

Women and children first, they said.

To which Spencer replied, "tough fuckin' titty!"

He burst out into the dark park and almost slammed right into a bunch of people gathered near the building. With a crazy arms-flailing yelp, he tried to leap straight backwards while still running full-tilt straight ahead.

As a result, his feet shot sideways on dew-damp grass, flipping him half a cartwheel and landing him on his side in a jarring impact. A split-second later, Beth, who'd been steamrollering along damn near up his ass, kidney-kicked him, tripped over him, and went fuckin' flying like Supergirl.

In the moment before she bellyflopped, the screen-glow of her phone illuminated a group of straggle-bearded bums in ratty coats. Then, wha-boom, she was down too, breath exploding in a whoof. Her phone spun a ways further through the grass and came to rest almost at the bums' toes, underlighting them like gantry-zombie-scarecrows from a scary movie.

Oh his fuckin' kidney oh that fuckin' hurt!

Spencer almost wished he'd gone ahead and pissed himself in terror while they were still below in Vault 420. Embarrassing as that would've been, at least then he wouldn't have been pissing blood…which he'd probably now be doing for the next week.

The bums, clutching depleted booze bottles in brown bags, nicotine stains on their fingers and scabs on their knuckles, made no aggressive moves. They just stood there, apprehensive but curious lookie-loos drawn by the ruckus.

"Sweet holy mother-of-god," one said. "What have you kids been up to?"

"What you kids *on*?" asked another. "Drugs're bad shit,

dontcha know?"

"Should stick t' booze an' smokes, better for ya," said the third. "Got a cig? Rollies? How 'bout a butt? Or a dollar? Ya got a dollar?"

"Shut it, Al." The first one, tall and skinny, bald as a baby's ass, shuffled a concerned step forward. "You all okay there?"

"We're fine," came Jake's voice. In that tone guys used after any stunt gone wrong; didn't matter if they had fuckin' broken *bones* sticking through their skin. "We're cool. It's all good."

"The fuck we are!" Spencer heard himself reply, his own voice a thin, pained wheeze. "Did you *see* that fuckin' thing? What the *fuck*?!"

Beth groaned as if stunned, then rolled into a crab-walk scuttle, trying to look everywhere at once. "Where is it? Where the hell *is* it? Did it follow us?"

The second bum, who'd cautioned them about drugs, nodded sagely. "On some bad shit, a'right. Must be."

"We're okay," Jake said. "We're okay, c'mon, chill."

"You think someone's been following you?" said the skinny baby-ass-bald one.

He sounded like he was trying to talk down the nutjobs, an impression strengthened by the way his buddy Al stood back and shared twirlyfinger-at-the-temple gestures with the fourth, a small pudgy guy lost in an oversized parka. The parka's hood, trimmed with a mangy crust of fake fur, was pulled up to hide most of his head, but Spence was pretty sure he could see the dull gleam of crumpled tinfoil as he indicated silent emphatic agreement with Al.

When the local literal tinfoil-hatters thought you were nutjobs…

Though maybe the local literal tinfoil-hatters had a point.

He did not feel, right now, like a sane and stable person.

Okay, so he rarely did, but this was fuckin' different!

"It's gonna get us oh jeez oh jeez don't let it get us it got Brendan didn't it did you see it got him what did it do to him what did it dooooo?" That was Devon, the new kid, hugging himself, dancing in place, gibbering like he was about to cry. At least, until Jake stepped up, caught him by the upper arms, and gave him a shake. "Dev!"

"Did it get him? Where is he?"

"Dev, chill, huh?"

"Leave him alone," huffed Marty, collapsing onto the bench of a wooden picnic table. "Leave him alone, huh? He's freaked, and can you blame him? Seriously, what the hell?"

"Where *is* Brendan?" Beth asked. "Oh shit, he isn't still down there, is he?"

"Fuck him if he is!" Spencer staggered upright, hands pressed to the small of his back like a goddamn geezer. "His fuckin' problem!"

"Whatever trouble you're in," said the first bum, still in that talk-down-the-psychos way, "I'm sure it's nothing to work yourselves up over. Take a minute, some deep breaths, and tell us what's wrong."

"Crap's sake, Nelson," Al said to him. "Ya wanna play group therapy, go on ahead, but me and Howie wants none of it."

Again, the silent one with the crumpled tinfoil skullcap under his hood agreed emphatically. The two of them retreated to watch from a distance.

"Me neither," said drugs-are-bad-m'kay. "They're on some mean shit. Maybe dangerous. Maybe those bath-salts, turn kids into zombies."

"We're not on fuckin' bath-salts!"

He squinted at Spencer. "Hang on. You Hannah Bodean's boy?"

Spence bristled. "The fuck is it to you if I am?"

Again, the sage nod. "Meth, then. That'd 'splain' it."

Kidneys? What kidneys? What pain? "Listen to me, you shithead old fuck, I'm gonna feed you your own ass and—"

Beth grabbed him before he got more than a couple steps in his rabid-weasel lunge at Mr. Just-Say-No.

Baby-bald Nelson put himself between them, hands held up, knobby wrists and several inches of scarred forearms showing below his threadbare cuffs. "Let's not have a problem, here, all right? Tater meant no offense."

"Tater? His name's fuckin' *Tater*?! Fuckin' *Mashed* Tater when I'm—"

"Get lost, would you?" Beth shouted at the bums.

"We're going. See? Going now. Come on, Tater. Let's go."

They went, and at a good goddamn clip, too. As they should. Shit-talk *his* mother? Yeah, they *better* fuckin' hustle!

When the bums and their scum-bum butt-buddies had vanished behind the bleachers to their shitty shanty-town, the blunt corkscrew of pain twisted into Spencer's kidney again. He hissed through his teeth.

Beth released him, but looked ready to grab again if he showed any signs of haring off after Tater. He attempted, with vague handwaves, to indicate he was cool, he was cool.

Jake released Devon, who also seemed to have gotten his shit semi-together. Marty heaved himself off the bench. Nobody saying anything. It was like fuckin' shellshock or something, all five of them.

Five. Still only five.

Slowly, they turned to look back the way they'd come, at the concrete building housing the restrooms.

There was no sign of Brendan.

Suddenly, Jake smacked himself in the forehead and cried aloud, "Oh, that son of a bitch!" In response to their baffled looks, he elaborated. "You guys thought *I* was pulling some stupid trick or joke. But it wasn't me. I really believed..."

"What?" asked Beth.

He shook his head. "Forget it, it's too dumb. Point is, the one who was fucking with us was *him*! Brendan! Must've been!"

"Huh?" said Devon.

"That dickbag bastard!" Spencer said. "I bet you're right! I bet he's down there right now, laughing his ass off!"

Marty frowned. "So, it *was* a trick?"

"Well, what else could it be?" Jake kicked disconsolately at a clump of weeds. "Damn it. I feel like such an idiot."

67

"That's because you are," Beth said. "But what's the deal? What do you mean? You can't have sincerely expected that demon-summoning shit to work."

His shoulders slumped. "Yeah, I guess."

"Wait, wait, whoa," Marty said. "Brendan did all that? With the candles and the special effects? The stinkbombs? Oh, man! I almost puked! And that...that...*thing*...that whatever-the-fuck-that-was?"

"You know it, the smarmy ass-licking fuckstick." Spencer glared in the direction of the restrooms, fists clenched as if he might give Brendan a double helping of the knuckle sandwiches Beth hadn't let him serve Tater.

Fuckin' *Tater*! The alky-wino-boozer D.A.R.E. bum.

"But why?" asked Devon. Poor dumbshit new kid, still wanting to think the best of everybody. Look who he hung out with, for fuck's sake! "I mean, there's joking around, yeah, but..."

"That was too far," Beth said. "Way too damn far. I knew he was a douche, I've been saying so forever. This, though, this takes the douche cake."

"We could've got hurt," said Marty.

"Could've?" Spence pressed the small of his back again. "Speak for yourself, Mart-O. Bethany here playin' fuckin' kickball with my kidneys—"

"It was an accident! And in case you didn't notice, I damn near killed myself tripping over your klutzy ass!"

"Look," said Jake. "It wasn't me. I sure don't think it was any of you guys; you were as freaked out as I was."

"Were?" said Marty.

"Are. Whatever. But it makes sense now. He's the one whose dad had all those movies, he helped me do a lot of the internet research, he's got money—"

"To rent or buy a creature-feature nightmare-fuel monster *that* good?" Beth's pierced eyebrow hoisted in a skeptical slant. "I don't know, Jake."

"C'mon, it wasn't *that* good," said Spencer, lying out his ass and fooling nobody. It *had* been good, it'd been fuckin' *convincing*.

Of course, they'd all been pretty hyped up, too. Adrenaline and suggestibility, *Paranormal Activity* bullshit, their own damn imaginations sucked them right in. Watch, it *would* turn out to be latex and foam rubber, no scarier than a Halloween decoration.

"And the way it went for him, right for him, just for *him*," Jake continued. "Then he could put on his screaming it's-got-me act."

Which had also been fuckin' *convincing*. Who knew the rich boy prick had any talent?

"So, where is he, then?" Devon gestured around. "Why hasn't he come out yet to laugh in our faces?"

"He's probably waiting for us to come back down all embarrassed," Marty said.

"Or," said Beth, "when we do, he's there pretending to be dead or something, hoping to zing us *again*, like a douche. *Then* laugh in our faces."

"Laugh his fuckin' ass off, bust a gut," Spencer said.

"Well...so...what do we do?" Devon asked.

"Hey, screw it," said Marty. "I'm not going back. He can clean up his own mess."

"Damn right," Beth said.

"Yeah," agreed Spencer. "Yeah, let him deal with it; I'm done. When he texts us later, all butthurt, I say we tell him to fuck the hell off."

"Damn right," Beth said again. "Do *not* need his shit."

"Seems kind of mean to just walk away, though."

"You can go find him if you want," Jake said. "I'm with Spence and Beth. What a clusterfuck."

"My mom's windchime—"

"Can fuckin' wait 'til tomorrow!" Spencer said.

Jake nodded. "I need to get those silver dishes back, too, but yeah. Tomorrow. For now, I just want to go home."

CHAPTER NINE
INEBRIATION

Howie found a flashlight in his shopping cart. Took some rummaging to dig it out, mixed in as it was amid a box of scavenged electronics odds-and-ends. Man had about nine miles of assorted wires, everything from power strips to strings of old Christmas bulbs to the twisty cord off a telephone.

But, he *did* find the flashlight.

A blue train-shaped plastic one where the light beamed from the front of some dopey-looking cartoon face. Still, it worked.

They waited until the group of kids who'd come caterwauling-ass-hauling up from the bunker had shoved off, then waited a while longer to make sure they weren't coming back.

While waiting, they shared around a couple 40-ouncer cans, a quart-sized box of what Nelson called 'cardbordeaux,' and a fifth of no-name-brand popskull Tater had in his pack.

Then, fortified and emboldened and curious, they trooped on down to see what they could see. Like the bear going over the mountain.

Normally, they steered clear of the bunker complex below the park. Sure, it might've made a decent camp, secure against wind and weather, out of sight of cops either of the well-meaning or asshole variety…but none of them liked being closed in.

Too much like prison. Too much like the state hospital.

Underground. Dank. Echoey.

Too many ways to get cornered. Too many ways to get lost or locked in or trapped.

Nelson said it was closter-fobic.

Al said it was damn spooky.

Like a dungeon. Like a basement. Like a tomb.

Or, like what it really was, which was the *real* issue to worry about.

Government installation.

The disused defense bunker thing could be just a cover story. A cover story for military bases and secret labs. The fact there was still power to some of the lights and water in some of the taps proved somebody must be up to something.

Well, they'd get more than they bargained for if they tried to mess with him. He was wise to their tricks.

He patted his parka hood as he followed Al's careful both-hands-on-the-handrails one-foot-two-foot stairwell descent. The foil cap—six layers of it, the heavy-duty kind, a roll he'd tucked under his coat while helping after-dinner cleanup at a soup kitchen over in Winston City—made a comforting squish-crinkle against his matted, oily hair.

Nobody would be reading *his* mind, and it wasn't as if they could make him talk, either. Not a single word in, what, thirty, forty years? However long it'd been since the babysitter told him what she'd do if he said anything to anyone, ever ever again.

Behind him, Tater muttered indignantly, something to do with how it hardly was *his* fault, now, was it; if the Bodean boy couldn't handle some simple home-truths. Hadn't meant anything by it, just honest statement of fact, no reason to go flying off the handle.

And behind Tater, bringing up the rear, Nelson reminded them all how they were only having a look around. He wanted to know what those kids had been doing, what'd gotten them in such a state. Not to land themselves in any trouble. Not to touch stuff, take stuff, break stuff.

Only to have a look around.

"Yeah, yeah," went Al, stumbling not because of the steps but because he'd reached the bottom and couldn't seem to cope with level floor. He fished a crumpled empty pack of generics from his pocket, peered into it as if the Cig Fairy had visited since last time he looked, sighed, and put it away again. "'less they left some smokes."

"I've no doubt they were smoking something, sure

enough," Nelson said, turning his shiny bald head this way and that like a skinny eagle. "I can smell it."

Howie took an experimental sniff, but all he got was his own usual dull and sour funk. He tried to calculate how long it'd been since he changed clothes, and couldn't. A lady who said she was with a church outreach group had tried a few weeks ago to coax him into letting her take him to the laundrymat, wash a few loads, wash his parka at least, but he'd seen right through her nice-seeming act.

"Had to've been more'n smokin' to account for the way they carried on. Meth or zombie salts or worse, I betcha. Ruinin' their lives with that bad shit." Tater paused for a long swig from a brown-bagged bottle, then covered his mouth with the back of one hand to half-stifle a belch.

"Lights thataway." Al, swaying, pointed like he was making the infinity sign in the air. "Brighter'n these ol' yellers." He set off in that direction, more or less, the way a slow-rolled bowling ball made its way along a lane with the bumpers up.

They trailed after him at their own gaits and paces, Howie casting shrewd covert glances at ceiling-mounted 'sprinklerheads' and other innocuous-looking fixtures no doubt cleverly concealing spy cams and microphones.

Watching. Listening. Probably content to do just that… for now…not wanting to give themselves away.

The lights Al had spotted were small, but definitely brighter than the yellow bulb above the doorway through which they issued. A couple of thin, conical beams, more like penlights than Howie's choo-choo ray.

The room they shone from was, even by the standards of people who lived in the park, a mess. Whatever those kids had been up to, they'd trashed the place and for sure. Congealed glop and ashes everywhere, reminding Howie of the time at the soup kitchen when the big pressure cooker exploded. Pork and beans from hell to Harvard, damn near burned down the building.

Al took a single step inside before Nelson collared him by the scruff and yanked him to a halt, making him bark indignantly.

"Look," Nelson said. His pointing was somewhat steadier than Al's had been. Somewhat. The outline on the floor was like the writing on the wall; once you saw it, you couldn't very well unsee it.

"Bad shit," Tater said. "Bad shit, bad news, I toldya so. They wasn't just druggin'. This is bad juju black magic shit."

"Them plates look real silver, though." Al squirmed and slapped ineffectually at Nelson's grip. "Hock shop guy I know, betcha he give us twenny, maybe fiddy—"

Nelson twisted his fist in Al's shabby collar. "And when those kids get past what scared them and come looking, what do you think they'll give you?"

Tater vehemently wagged his head. "I ain't settin' foot and won't have no part of devil-money off'n witch-silver or drugs."

"Dumb drunk fools th' both ya. Howie?"

Howie waved his hands back and forth in front of his chest, signaling his own no-thanks. Not that he was religious or superstitious, but he knew a set-up, some kind of trick or test, when he saw it.

He turned from the room with its pressure-cooker aftermath residue, scanning the hallway in hopes of detecting the tell-tale glint of a spy-cam lens. Behind one of the vents in the wall, most likely, was his guess.

Further down the hall, a faint greenish-blue glimmer spilled around a corner. Something liquidy and weirdly familiar about it sent a mingled chill and thrill out of nowhere across the nape of Howie's neck.

It reminded him of…of…

Ripple-bubble-gurgle-glow.

Something horrible. Something he hated.

Something he used to love.

"Hey, check't out!" Al said. "Think that's one-a them hippie lamps. Ain't seen one in years! Used'ta have one in my room'n I was fi'teen." He paused, and grinned. "First time I got laid, by that light."

Was this it? The start of another experiment? They'd avoided the obvious trap of the room with the occult setup, but now here was this light. This eerie, fluid, familiar, awful light.

"A lava lamp?" Nelson frowned. "No, it's more like… there's no…pool down here, is there? A swimming pool?"

"Down here?" Al snorted. "Y'all're wasted. Hippie lamp, I'm tellin' ya."

The glimmer, the glow, spilling and spreading, brighter, strengthening.

And yes, the sounds, the burbling sloosh and slush, low, constant, steady.

As shapes flitted and shadows flicked. Through feathery strands, curves and coves and caves and outcrops. Colorful pebbles. Pearly beads rising from a sunken ship.

The cool blue-green light, playing soft through the glass in the darkened living room.

He would look at the fish. He would look at the fish.

He loved the fish in their big aquarium-tank.

Used to love the fish.

He would look at the fish until it was over.

Count them, if he could.

Bright little fish. Tetras, they were called. Guppies. Stripey ones he didn't know the name.

Looking at the fish.

Not looking at the babysitter. At what the babysitter was doing.

Not looking, but feeling.

Unable not to feel.

*If you tell…if you tell anyone, ever…if you say anything to anyone, ever, **ever**…*

"Went to Hawaii once't," Tater said, in a dreamy but choked-up kind of way. "Fr'our honeymoon. She were so beautiful."

He and Al shuffled a few dreamy paces forward. Toward the strengthening blue-green glimmer. Like it was a good thing.

Nelson hesitated, scrubbing his palm over his bald pate. "Swim team." He did not look or sound dreamy. He looked and sounded pained. "I was good. They said I had real potential. Olympic potential."

74

Howie tilted his foil-capped, hooded head. All these years and had he ever heard Tater mention a wife? Nelson being a swimmer? He didn't think so, didn't remember, but he couldn't focus his mind, couldn't.

Then, sighing like a sob, sobbing like a sigh, Nelson followed Tater and Al.

Howie felt his own feet start to move along with them. He tried to stop himself short.

A grimy tear trickled into Tater's beard. "Oh if you'd've seen her...bikini and sun-hat with this flowered skirt-wrap thing tied on her hips...we took a sail on a glass-bottom boat...never been happier."

No. No no no.

A bad thing.

He hadn't told. Hadn't told anyone, ever! Hadn't said anything to anyone, ever, *ever*!

"I was so afraid they'd...they'd find me out," Nelson went on. "The other..." He drew a deep, shuddery breath. "Boys. They'd see how I...they'd know what I..."

The babysitter.

If you do, if you tell your mom, your dad, anyone, if you say anything to anyone ever, **ever**, *I'll get you. I'll hurt you. I'll hurt* **them**. *I'll hurt them, and it'll be all your fault. Your fault.*

Nelson kept talking, though Howie was only half-aware of his words. One day, after practice, stayed late, another boy, Eric, so smooth, smooth and taut, lean and perfect, and Eric *had* known—

"Hey, ya smell that?" asked Al, from further down the hallway. "Smells like pizza! Hot pizza extra cheese!"

"Nah, 's biscuits," Tater said. "Buttermilk biscuits fresh from t'oven."

"Hell ya say; it's pizza."

The blue-green light played its underwater flicker-dance over their faces, dazzling in their eyes like kaleidoscope jewels.

"Popcorn," said Nelson. "Movie theater popcorn. We went to the movies. We could do that, it wouldn't seem strange, a couple of friends going to the movies. Side by side in the dark. Arms touching. Knees. Just sitting together, eating popcorn."

Howie smelled, above or through his own unwashed funk, a whiff of warmth and deliciousness.

Not popcorn, not pizza, not biscuits; they were all wrong. It was pancakes. Thick, fluffy pancakes. Like his mom would make, Sunday mornings, after she and Daddy had their night out, their night when the babysitter came over.

The fish, swimming endless loops and laps and circles and figure-eights in their watery fish-world, their silent and bubbling fish-world, ripples of turquoise and shadow on gravel, on glass, secret hollows in rocks and coral.

The fish and he'd loved them, he hated them, the fish who did nothing, who ignored it, or who watched and saw and didn't help.

And Mom made pancakes, stacks and stacks of them, pancakes with syrup, and what was the matter with little Howie, why was he so quiet today, did he feel all right, was he sick, was he upset, what's wrong Howie?

Howard answer your mother answer your father why isn't he talking should we call the doctor what is it honey you can tell us he just sits there and won't say a word won't make a sound he hears us I know he hears us he listens he does what we ask him to everything except talk why won't he talk?

Then they rounded the corner and saw what was there, what filled the hallway, oozing and dripping. They saw the pulsing growths bulging from it, opening, inviting, extending long supple tendrils toward them.

They saw what was suspended in its grasping, slithering, undulous midst—

They heard the noises, the grunts and slurp-smacks and gobbles.

Howie felt his knees just unlock, his body just go boneless. He felt the hot gush-flood wetness of piss soaking his pants.

He felt a peeling, tearing, stinging pain. In his throat. Inside his throat. He tasted, gagged, and choked on thin trickles of blood.

"Babysitter!" Howie screamed. "Babysitter! Babysitter!"

INTERLUDE: VIGNETTES #3

Well, that kind of went to some darker places in more ways than one. Supposed throw-away comic relief characters having their own poignant backstories and stuff, what the hell's up with that?

***

And meanwhile, what's in store for poor Brendan? After all, if you remember back in the prologue, he wasn't even with the other four guys. Some foreshadowing for ya there.

Along with some other mysteries and unresolved secrets. Jake has some kind of secret ace-in-the-hole mystery going on, which he hadn't wanted to mention up front in case it didn't pan out...but, by the looks of it, something sure did!

What our young heroes—or, our bunch of retards, as Beth would say—have summoned in Vault 420 *is*, in fact, a succubus. They did it. They summoned a demon.

Beware of what you wish for, am I right?

Hot naked demon chicks with little cute bat wings and tails, indeed. Shape-shifting psychic love-slaves, yeah right.

Just your basic adolescent horndog sex-fantasies.

Honestly, it's like with mermaids. The notion of big bare buoyant boobs, flowing gorgeous hair, and all the fellatio a guy could ever hope for, but without any of that squicky vagina business. Complicated parts and how weird they might look/smell/taste, and performance anxiety and women are so difficult to please. And let's not start on the menstrual phobias or the entitlement issue debates about personal grooming.

Reality can be such a disappointment, can't it?

There's more than a few folks in Fairmont who could speak to that point...

***

Hank Vilstreet drags himself home after another seventeen-hour shift. He parks in the driveway and sits there a minute, waiting for his favorite song to finish up on the radio, before going in.

House is dark and quiet. No surprise there. Carla had called him earlier to let him know she was laid low with one of her migraines. The dinner she'd promised—her special chicken and dumplings—would have to wait. But he could heat himself up a can of stew or make a sandwich or something, couldn't he?

He's a foreman at *Le Prestige du Vin* winery, a hard-won promotion he'd thought—more fool he!—would mean more respect and less scut-work.

What it really means, he's discovered, is that if anything goes wrong, it's his ass. If anything doesn't get done, it's his ass.

The vats didn't get hosed out? There's a mix-up with the timesheets? Mis-labeled bottles? Worker's comp issues and union grievances? Someone smoking by the loading dock again? A 'spill' in the tasting room?

Hank will take care of it.

Hank will take care of everything.

Why else would he merit a token bump in salary and a spiffy little gold-tone pin to wear on his coveralls?

His house may be dark, but a few lights are still on over at Coach's place. Coach Lewis Bodean, one of his neighbors. They even used to be buddies, of a sort. Buddies, until Hank just couldn't take any more of his talk.

Sure, he means well, Coach does, in his way. He means well, but there are limits to how much Hank can listen to about how men were being suckered and strung along. Even with sufficient beer, there are limits.

No use arguing with him, either. He'd just accuse Hank of playing ostrich, head in the sand, digging in and doubling down. The willful obtuseness of the hopelessly pussy-whipped.

As if Coach could possibly understand.

The song finishes, the DJ comes on with some blather, and Hank cuts him short. He goes up the walk, up the steps, opens the door. Careful steps, avoiding the creaky spots, finding his way by familiarity more than sight. The air's kind of stale, kind of musty. Needs a good hard cleaning and airing out.

Maybe, next time he has a day off…

Or, maybe they could look into one of those maid services?

Not that he can afford it, even with the pay bump. Not until he's paid down the credit cards a bit.

Reaching the kitchen, he flips the switch. The light over the sink shows him their breakfast dishes—he cooked eggs—sitting in cold soap-filmy water. Plates, the egg pan, coffee cups. Plus a spinach-flecked bowl and cutting board, from which he deduces Carla had salad for lunch.

The migraine must've come on later in the afternoon, then. He finds the chicken in the freezer, not thawed in the fridge; she probably put it back when she realized she wouldn't be feeling up to cooking.

Hank runs the hot tap until the dishwater foams. He washes, dries, wipes the counters, takes out the trash. All hardly half thinking about it. A can of stew, even a sandwich, seems like too much extra work. Some crackers and sliced cheese will do him fine.

He eats, then goes down the hall with the same quiet care to avoid the creaky places. By the glow of the digital clock, he can just make out the Carla-shaped lump under the covers. She doesn't stir. He can hear her slow, even breathing.

In the bathroom, he shuts the door before turning on the light, and as he goes about the routine bedtime tasks of undressing and brushing his teeth, he notices a box from one of the fancy downtown boutiques sitting amid her usual clutter of cosmetics.

Its lid is ajar, revealing tissue paper and the frilly edge of something delicate. He peeks. Silky pink, with milky lace. He can just imagine how she'd look in it, how it'd drape and cling and flatter.

His poor, dear Carla. She'd obviously meant to be waiting for him tonight, with a home-cooked meal and something special for dessert. But, instead, another migraine had to come along and ruin everything.

It had been a long time, too. Since…

Their anniversary? His birthday? The night of his promotion?

No, not then; he remembered how his bosses took them out for a celebratory dinner and she'd been so proud of him, so cuddly and affectionate, he'd been sure they would…until her headache got its claws in on the drive back to the house.

She'd offered anyway, he remembered that, too. Of course he couldn't take her up on it. How shit-selfish would that have been? And she'd promised to make it up to him.

Clearly, she'd hoped to make it up to him tonight.

Maybe, he thinks as he slides gingerly into his side of the bed, trying not to jostle her, he should stop and pick her up some flowers tomorrow. She deserves them. He's a lucky, lucky man.

***

Cynthia-Lynne Abbott, that blonde beauty with not much in the way of tits but legs like holy-Judas-whoa, is really liking what Troy's doing.

This time, she thinks, she might actually get there.

But, before she can, she feels what else he's trying to do. On the sly. Like she won't notice. Like she can't tell the difference between rubbing fingers and a probing, naked dick.

She pushes him away, smacks him on the chest. "Troy, I said *no!*"

At least he doesn't give her the confused innocent act. He flops over onto his back, with a big disgruntled expulsion of breath.

"God damn it, Cyn, what's the matter, why not?"

"I've told you!"

"Saving yourself, yeah, but for what?"

80

"Until I'm sure. Until I'm ready."

"We've been going together *how* long?"

"Off and on," she reminds him, a well-honed edge in her voice.

"Okay, okay, look, I'm sorry."

It's the same conversation they've had before, the same song-and-dance so well-rehearsed it could be a vaudeville routine. She's just so hot, so sexy, he wants to be close to her, it makes him crazy, is that so wrong? While she maintains there are plenty of other things they can do, plenty of other ways to enjoy each other, why does he have to be hung up on *that*?

What she suspects, though, is if she lets him have *that*, he'll lose interest. She's binge-watched *The Tudors*. She's seen the way her playboy uncle goes through women. She listens to cautionary musical laments by Adele and Taylor Swift and Lorde.

The eager, kindling, close-to-climax rush in her loins is lukewarm history. She swings those holy-Judas-whoa long legs out of his bed and goes looking for her panties. Which she'd intended to keep on, but she'd finally convinced him to do the slow firm circular pressure instead of jabbing at the button like someone impatient for an elevator, and it had been feeling so fantastic and she hoped he might let it be about *her* for a change, not about him or his hardon or his prowess and bragging rights.

No such luck. He'd had to go and try to sneak it into her—bareback, no less, when they'd also had plenty of *those* discussions before—and ruin everything.

Sometimes she wishes he wasn't so annoyingly rich and handsome and perfect. Or less of an arrogant asshole. Why couldn't there be more guys who were both nice *and* confident and attractive? Real-nice, not Nice-nice.

Panties, check. Wispy silk whispers up slim thighs. She starts gathering the rest of her clothes. Troy lounges there in the rumpled sheets, looking like he's posing for a hook-up site. He hasn't bothered to readjust the briefs he'd eased down, as if hoping the sight of his still-semi will change her mind.

It isn't fair. She wants to, she *does*! This whole staying-a-virgin thing is a colossal pain. But she isn't going to be anybody's conquest, anybody's fuck-and-dump, like Uncle Sebastian's ongoing list of been-there-done-thats.

Troy says, "So, you're leaving?" and she says she guesses she'd better, and he tells her hey not to be mad, and she contemplates telling him to f.o.a.d., but she can't and she doesn't, and they do the usual closing routine of who'll text whom later, so it isn't another of their break-ups, and she drives herself home.

On the way, she passes Vintner's Green, the golf course, dark and quiet in the middle of the night.

It makes her think of that one guy who works there, Marty's friend, Jake. She's seen him out there lugging golf bags, groundskeeping, driving the little carts. He's got a cute smile, and an even cuter butt. He looks like he'd be a good kisser.

Good at other things, too.

She's still thinking along those lines when, after turning out the light and setting her phone on the nightstand, she slides both hands under the covers to finish herself off.

Mmmm. Jake. Oh, ooh yes. Touching her, kissing her, doing it right.

Maybe she should ask Marty about him some time.

Smiling, Cynthia-Lynne drifts into contented sleep.

CHAPTER TEN
CONFESSION

"So," said Beth, "you never did tell us why you thought that crazy demon-summoning shit might actually work."

Jake, with an abashed grin, coughed and looked away. "I…yeah…well…it was dumb."

"Obviously, but what was it?"

They were in the apartment, him at his computer, her kicking back on the couch, and Devon taking a turn in the gaming chair because Marty was stuck working a late shift at the Shop-N-Go. Spencer wasn't around for a change, being off helping some relative or another with something it was best not to know about on the grounds it might be incriminating.

As for Brendan…

He'd show up eventually, Jake figured. Text them or drop by, acting like nothing had happened, or all butthurt because they couldn't take a joke. In the meantime, none of them had seen or heard from him since that night in Vault 420, and it was just as well.

"Fuck him, anyway, the fuckin' fuckstick," Spence had said, a sentiment with which the rest of them were inclined to agree.

"I always said he was a douche."—Beth.

"That totally wasn't funny."—Marty.

Like quotes from movie reviewers. So what if the guy had money and a car? They didn't need him to buy their damn pizza. He *was* a fuckstick douche, and the stunt he'd pulled *hadn't* been funny.

As far as Jake was concerned, Brendan could shove it. Made him look stupid in front of his friends, his posse, his crew…yeah, thanks a lot, Brendan, thanks a lot, go to hell.

Even if, okay, it hadn't *all* been on Brendan. Jake himself

83

had to own up to his own share in the looking-stupid thing. He sighed, seeing Beth giving him an impatient and skeptical pierced-eyebrow hoist.

"You know my granddad, the one who was big into local history?"

She nodded. "Who told you about Shelter Park and everything, yeah."

"He also got into genealogy the last year or so before he died. Family trees and that stuff."

"Like we had to do in third grade? I remember that. Mrs. Sharpe, what a bitch."

"Only, further back, like, way back. He traced ours, on his side, his mom's side, and…oh, damn it, it *is* dumb, let's just forget it."

"No way. Spill."

He sighed again. "Okay, okay. So, he traced it back, way back, and found out that his mom's grandmother, which would be my…great-great-great-grandma, I think…anyway, she was…"

Jeez it felt even dumber saying it aloud, but they were both looking at him, waiting expectantly for his answer. Devon had paused his game—not *Hellslayer*, just a cheap *Call of Duty* knockoff first-person shooter Marty'd picked up on sale.

"Her name was Temperance Nachtwald," Jake said.

Devon's expression only went more confused, but Beth gawped at Jake a second and then flung back her head to whoop a loud laugh.

"Sssst!" he hissed, jerking a thumb toward the wall.

Beth reined in the laugh, but with effort. "The crazy lady who poisoned all those kids?"

"No! That…" He glanced down again, the shame-blush once more burning hot in his face. "… that was her sister."

"Wait. Wait." She sat up straighter on the couch and leaned forward, elbows on knees. "Are you seriously telling me that, because your granddad connected your family with the weirdo witches of Blackwell Hill…"

"Weirdo witches?" asked Devon, now beyond confused

and into totally lost. "What?"

"Back in pilgrim times, two hundred years ago or whatever," Beth said. "Hexes and curses and burning people at the stake."

"That happened *here*?"

"It happened lots of places," Jake said. "Only, the Nachtwalds, they, well, everyone believed they were the real deal."

"And you thought..." Beth snorted another laugh into her curled fist. "You thought being related to them meant you had magic powers? Our own half-assed Harry Potter?"

"I know, I *know*! It was stupid, okay? The whole thing was stupid. Look, can't we please forget about it? When I went back down for the plates and Dev's mom's windchime and stuff—"

"Yeah, thanks, she would have wondered," Devon said.

"—I got rid of the candles, kicked around and stirred up the ashes and salt. It's a mess in there, yeah, especially the dried goo from whatever silly-string crap Brendan set off, but you can't tell what was going on."

"That's good," Beth said. "Anybody hassle you?"

"No, didn't see anyone."

The bums hadn't even been around, though of course it'd been the middle of the day, which probably meant they'd taken their PLEASE HELP GOD BLESS cardboard signs to whichever spots they'd staked out. Vault 420 itself had smelled like burnt toast and ass, and the signature clock must've been jarred when it fell from the wall to smack Spence on the head; its hands now stuck at more like 5:35.

Definitely no longer a cool place to go.

In fact, Jake would be perfectly happy to never visit Shelter Park again, let alone what was under it.

Being down there had still given him some residual creeps, but the creeps were more than overshadowed by embarrassment. Embarrassment, humiliation, anger, and shame. If he *had* run into Brendan, Jake might have kicked his ass.

He almost could've sworn, as he stuffed the ruined

papers, the chewed plastic dog-dish, and other junk into a trash bag, he'd heard whispers from the darker reaches of the bunker's halls. Whispers and snickers, mocking, laughing, making fun. *Hey look, there's one of those dink-brains who tried to summon a demon.*

Yeah, real funny. Hilarious.

Of the monster-leech-bug-thing, there'd been no sign. Brendan must have taken it with. Probably cost him plenty. Probably, he'd try to spring it on them again at some point, and then Jake really *would* kick his ass.

There was also the matter of the damn video. Beth had sent it to the rest of them, but not posted it yet. As far as Jake knew, none of them had watched it yet either; nobody was in a hurry to see how fucking stupid they looked, screaming and freaking out.

Jake was also concerned about what it might show of *him*. Beth wouldn't have zoomed in for a close-up, but he'd made it this far in his life without having his dick on the internet, and he'd really prefer to keep it that way.

That he'd *done* it…

In front of his friends. In front of Beth and the guys.

At the time, in the moment, it hadn't been about sex, or lust, or pleasure. Nothing like that. What mattered right then hadn't been any ultimate goal of naked nympho devil-chicks. What mattered was the ritual. The *power*. Bending the forces of magic and nature to his will.

God, what a complete and utter moron he'd been.

This was how people got swept up in and carried away by crazy cult shit.

Devon and Beth left before midnight. Jake sat at his computer a while longer, trying to decide what to do, what to watch, what to play. Nothing held his interest. When he realized he was so bored and distracted he was contemplating cleaning the apartment, he decided the best option was to say screw it, and go to bed.

Not that sleep proved within easy reach, either. For a change, the behemoth next door with the neck-tats and the temper was the one who could stand to lower the volume—

something with a laugh-track, canned and phony, forced, overdone.

When he finally did start to drift off, it was into a vague, drifty half-there half-dream of floating...or flying... or swimming...not falling, he knew that...the sense was of being both supported and weightless...surrounded freedom...a moving through without a pushing against...a slipping and gliding, slip-sliding, like from a song...

And someone was there with him.

Warm and aqua-blue.

A liquid, musical rippling...harpstring murmurs.

The shimmer. The glow.

Aqua-blue yes aqua-blue the shine of her eyes and her slow, lingering touch...

Intimate. Erotic.

Desire.

Yes. Desire and craving and urgency and *need.*

Needing him. Wanting him. To touch and to taste.

Her?

Why *her,* of all people? Of all girls? It was a dream, only a dream, a conscious corner of Jake's mind saw/knew/ recognized that, but strong enough of a conscious corner to let seep in senses of guilt, of betrayal.

Oh but she wanted him needed him to be with him to kiss and caress, here, now, like this, their secret their secret let her touch him let her taste him let her take him into herself her welcoming eagerness ready and moist and receptive and how good it felt, yes, to feel her curling and closing and clasping snug-hot-wet around him, and what she could *do,* the sensations, slick and coaxing, rhythmic pressure.

A dream but what a dream, what a dream, because no way in the real world no way any real girl let alone her let alone Cynthia-Lynne Abbott of all people and Marty was his friend, had been his friend since they were kids, not that she was Marty's girl or ever could be, Nice Guy or not, friendzone or not; maybe there were leagues and maybe there weren't but if there were, she was way out of Marty's, out even of Jake's, and he barely knew her to speak to, never

mind the other day at Vintner's Green when she'd been there
for brunch with her uncle and some of his big-shot rich hotel
friends and she'd made eye contact with him, eye contact
and a little smile and kind of a shoulder-wiggle with a finger
twining in her hair and Spence was right her legs in that hug-
sleek skirt holy-Judas-whoa and did that make *him* Judas,
betraying his friend?

But she wasn't Marty's girl. She was Troy-fucking-
Cahill's, if she was anybody's, wasn't she? Wasn't she?

But Marty loved her. Marty loved her and Marty would
die if Jake so much as said hi to Cynthia-Lynne Abbott, let
alone be here like this be here with her like this...

Be here with his cock in her mouth her head bobbing
her throat drawing his cockhead deep her tongue curling and
slip-gripping his shaft while her hair whispered damp silken
tendrils over his groin and thighs while she cradled and
fondled and rolled his balls in her mouth in her mouth her
lips there too her tongue circling his cock and also plying his
balls and slithering around them and under them worming
between his buttcheeks and tickling-nudging-teasing,
teasing and then easing, easing in, as her head bobbed her
lips suckled her tongues lapped and coiled and squeezed
and milked, sopping warm slurping mouths and throats
and tongues, cupping his balls and engulfing his cock and
delving squirmy-wormy up inside him...

So *good*, God *yes*, so goddamn *good*!

His hands reaching, reaching for her head, thinking to
stop her had to stop her oh so good but so *wrong* wasn't it
wrong why *her* why *him* why *now* why like *this*, not wanting
to stop her never wanting her to stop all the things she was
doing all her *mouths* and her *tongues* working him coaxing
him milking him how could he stop her when it felt so *good*
when he was *coming,* coming so *hard,* coming again and
again surge after gushing copious *surge* as she throated him
so deep so goddamn *deep* gulping and swallowing taking it
all gulping it down, and he couldn't stop her *wouldn't* stop her
wanted her *never* to stop, reaching for her to hold her there
to keep going keep going yes keep sucking licking drinking

take it *all* take *him* all drink him down drain him dry with his cock in her throat and her tongue in his ass and his balls in his mouth and his hands on her head, her head slippery and pulsating with her hair twining alive, those damp tendrils alive and moving, medusoid, undulating, *moving*!

A booming knock, a hard pounding, someone hammering on the wall. And a voice, an angry voice—*another* voice, because Jake also heard his own, his *own* voice raised in hoarse, grunting cries of orgasmic sex-throes, rutting and bestial fuck-noises from *him* as—

—he looked down through bleary-blinking eyes, through a warm and wavery aqua-blue glow, to see the dream was a nightmare, the bulbous wrinkled flesh and loose folds of the atrocity sprawled across his groin, its polyps flexing in time with the steady gulping suction of its innermost slick and fleshy contours, as its other orifices and protrusions rolled and probed and worked him with such hideously pleasurable sensations that he came *again*—

—and heard his shriek follow him down into oblivion.

CHAPTER ELEVEN
VISITATION

He is done.
Spent and sated.
Drained and spent.
He is done.
Milked of seed, the warm life-seed life-milk man-seed-milk, virile and rich, vibrant and teeming, the salt-cream-essence filling, fulfilling, to milk and drink, drink and swallow, gathering, good.
He who Called.
We are One-Many-All.
One-Many-All and now *Her*.
She hungers. She thirsts. She needs, commands, craves.
More.
More and more.
More to grow. More to become. To transform. To feed and to serve.
He is done.
He is young, he is strong.
Wait.
Wait and replenish. Wait and rest.
Or...
Another.
There are others.
Some who also Called. Invited and offered. Summoned. Who opened the way.
Who desire.
Desire the touch, the kiss and caress, the warm engulfment slick suction urging and urging to flood-gush-spill, spill the salt life-milk, copious, wriggling with seed.
To be swallowed, to fill, be fulfilled, and want more.
More until spent. More until done.

Until drained, until dry, until blood, until death?

The first.

Too much.

Mistake, mistake but the hunger, the craving, the thirst.

New and forming-unformed, still becoming.

Desperate, starving, unplaced, afraid.

Needing.

Needing to live, to survive, to be, to become.

Needing, and so, taking.

Taking and taking.

The first, as We-Many-One-All, rudely born-torn, pulled through, harsh and feeble, wet and flailing, Called into being.

Into this world-place, Called with purpose, with desire and intent, called by Will and by Word, the giving of sigils and symbols, fertility, Life.

Then, confusion. Then, uproar and upheaval.

Fear. Panic.

Need and Hunger, Hunger and Need.

To take.

Take and take.

Take to survive, live, be, grow.

To become.

Taking too much. Draining. Engulfing and encompassing, surrounding, absorbing, consuming.

Fluids.

Salt-sweat and salt-tears and salt-milk and salt-blood.

Juices of organs and marrow and mind.

Youth. Health. Virility.

Until dried. Until dead.

The relief. The release. The filling fulfillment.

Feeding the hunger. Quenching the thirst. Meeting the need.

Then, renewal. Then, purpose.

Craving more, needing more, to grow and become.

And so, seeking…

Others who did not Call, but found, found and saw, found and witnessed, saw and beheld.

Less-young and not-young.

Less virile, less healthy, less strong.

Sour fluids, pungent crustings, steeping, fermented, crowded-cluttered-chaotic cacophonies of thought.

Thoughts of maiden-woman-youth-man.

Liquid light.

Warmth and tantalizing aroma.

Comfort. Desire. Filled and fulfilled.

Lust-love-passion, guilt-shame-fear.

Fascinated. Compelled. Drawn and lured.

And *taken*.

Seized and taken, sweat-filth-crust-clothes, vile-bile, vomit, bowel and bladder, fungus and oil, sores-scabs-infection, earwax, warts and hair, mucus, parasites-lice-mites-bedbugs, but taken, taken and taken, subsumed-consumed and *used*, drained dry, drained to feed, to feed and grow, grow and thrive, grow and live-thrive-gain-become.

Many become One become All become *Her*.

And from Her, become Many/One.

One to go, to seek and search, search and find, find and answer.

Answer the Call.

He Who Called.

Summoned.

By Word and by Will and by Deed.

By offering of milk-salt-seed-life.

To find…to crave and need and feed…in his mind-thoughts his lust-thoughts…forbidden temptation irresistible… swollen stiffness rising engorged to be engulfed…groaning in pleasure, penetrating, being penetrated…again and again.

Until spent.

Until sated.

Until beyond arousal or erection.

Until done.

He is done.

But, more.

Nearby, another, others, and more.

CHAPTER TWELVE
TEMPTATION

"Know what really annoys me?" Beth said, as they walked up Rose Street. Rose-like-the-flower in this part of town, lined mostly with duplexes and small neighborhood businesses, buttoned up dark and quiet at this time of night.

Devon shot her a wary sidelong glance. "Do I have to pick just one thing?"

She laughed, nudge-bumping him with an elbow. "Good point. You're kinda funny when you stop trying so hard."

"Uh, thanks, I guess?"

"And kinda cute when you're confused."

"Uhhhh..."

She laughed again, and this time hip-bumped him. "Like that."

"So, um, okay...what really annoys you?"

Beth heaved a sigh and stuffed her fists wrist-deep into the pockets of her hoodie. The sporadic streetlamps they passed under cast pools of light and shadow over her face, making it impossible for him to read her expression.

"You *guys*," she said.

"Who? Me and Jake and them? Us guys? Or, guys in general, or what?"

"In general and or what. All through this, since the start of the succubus talk and everything, not once did...I mean, shit...did it even *occur* to any of you?"

"Did what occur to us?"

"That *I'm* a girl, numbnuts."

"Well..." Devon floundered around a little. "Yeah, but..."

"Yeah but I'm practically one of the guys? Yeah but not a *real* girl, not a hot babe, so it doesn't count?"

"I didn't say..."

"You didn't have to say. Nobody has to say. I can tell. I

don't look like them, I don't dress like them or act like them. The only reason Coach lets me hang out at his place is he figures I'm a lezzie."

"Uh…but…we know you're a girl; you're always giving us shit about guy-stuff…when Brendan brought that movie over—"

"Boobs and bush, aaaaaall natural, seventies vintage," she said. "Did you enjoy it?"

"I…it was…awkward."

"Embarrassing?"

"Yeah."

"You were blushing."

He didn't answer, but ducked his head because there he went again, the tingle flushing his face.

"But you did still enjoy it."

"Hey, if you were…offended or something…"

"Offended? Why, because I'm a girl and here's my friends sitting around watching porn, cracking jokes, being total oinking sexist pig assholes? Because I'm a girl and here's my friends talking about women as sex objects and wank-fodder and how they gotta get laid before they die of terminal blue balls, and the best solution they can think of is to try and summon a demon?"

Devon winced so hard it hurt. "When you put it that way, it sounds pretty shitty."

"It is pretty shitty."

"Jeez, Beth, I'm sorry."

"You should be. I may not be a damn Barbie doll but, what, am I invisible? How do you know I'm not a tight dress and a makeover away from being a knockout, like the plain dumpy gal-pal tomboy in the movies?"

The defensive thoughts scrambling around in his head did a sudden jumbling logjam derail. "What?"

"When you look at me," she said, stopping and gesturing at herself, "you see *this*, right? Bulky, unflattering clothes… tough-chick piercings, dyke haircut…but how do you know I don't have a dynamite bod under here?"

His eyebrows tried to tie in a knot and his jaw just sort of seesawed. Only inarticulate query-noises babbled from his mouth.

"Maybe it hurt my feelings that not one of you so much as asked," Beth said. "Maybe it's insulting to be ignored and overlooked, even when you're all going on about how desperate you are."

"I'm not—"

She unzipped her hoodie with a metallic purr. "I might," she said, "have the most amazing boobs you've ever seen in your life."

"Hey…whoa, wait…Beth!" Devon skittered back a step, raising his hands the way contestants did when the clock ran out on those chef shows.

"What's the matter, Devon? Scared?"

The hoodie dropped in a crumple to the sidewalk behind her. Under it, she wore an old black tee with the collar and sleeves cut away to turn it into a tattered tank top. The band logo on the front was a flaked and faded metallic turquoise; he couldn't decipher it, partly for the flaked-and-faded reason but mostly because…

"Uh…" he said. His eyebrows had stopped trying to tie knots and instead made high arches to accommodate eyes that felt about to telescope from his skull like a cartoon character's.

"I'm just saying," said Beth, gazing down at her chest, gripping the bottom of her shirt and tugging it tight, and taking a deep breath, "maybe you don't know what you've been missing."

"Yuh…err…umm…"

No bra. Cleavage. Nipples poking at thin cloth, further distorting the already distorted logo.

"Problem?" she asked, waggling her shoulders just enough to start a rocking-swaying—

Motion of the spheres, he thought.

No bra!

Boobs!

"Yo, Devon? Earth to Devon?"

"Huhhhhh?" With monumental effort, he dragged his

95

gaze—eyes up here!

She winked, and did a devilish half-grin with a peek of tongue-tip. "Wanna see my tattoo?"

"Uh…whuh…"

Beth trailed her fingers along the stretched neckline, then lower, tracing the curve of waist and hip—which were way curvier than he expected, *holy-hourglass-Batman* territory, those baggy jeans hid some serious *wow!*—to linger in the bikini-line vicinity.

"My tattoo, cutie," she repeated. "Wanna see it?"

***

Marty trudged the last half-mile from the bus stop, just wanting to get home and get some sleep. Another crappy night at the Shop-N-Go. The only good part had been chatting with Cynthia-Lynne Abbott, until even that went to shit.

She'd broken up with Troy again—Troy-fucking-Cahill—and Marty had played it cool, letting her vent, assuring her she was too good for Troy anyway, she deserved someone better, someone who'd treat her right, who'd appreciate the special and beautiful person she was. Should he stop by after work, maybe bring her that mint-chip ice cream she liked? He'd be glad to, it'd be no trouble at all.

Aww ur 2 sweet, she'd texted back, with a heart. And gone on to tell him thanks but not tonight, she was just going to take a long hot bubble bath and slide into bed… mental images that more than made up for any twinge of disappointment. They could, she said, chat more tomorrow.

Then came the nut-punch out of nowhere.

Did he know if that friend of his, Jake, was seeing anyone?

LOL blushyface winkyface blushyface j/k but not rlly

Critical hit.

All the way home, bus ride and trudge, with that replaying on a loop.

j/k but not rlly

He was really dragging ass by the time he reached the

apartment building. On his way up the stairs, he met their scary odd-hours neighbor, who was on his way out to…who knew, a casting call for extras in the next Mad Max movie, maybe.

"Hey," the behemoth said, in his deceptive-soft voice, "tell your buddy that it's great, you know, he's having girls over and whatever, getting lucky, that's cool, good for him… but the whole rest of the building doesn't need to hear it. Yeah?"

"I don't know what you're talking about, dude."

"Just tell him to tone it down. Other people need to sleep."

"Sure," said Marty. "Sure, I'll tell him."

"A'right. Seeya." Down the stairs he went.

Marty, somewhere between baffled and pissed, stood there watching him go.

The hell? Having girls over? As if it wasn't enough Cynthia-Lynne Abbott was checking Jake out, now Jake was also having girls over while he was at work?

Not only having girls over, but having noisy neighbor-waking sex into the bargain?

Dude.

He unlocked the door and opened it onto the usual clutter of their living room, dimly lit by the LED displays of various electronics. TV was off, computers hibernating, Jake's door shut.

But…

Stepping inside, Marty sniffed the air. Mingled with the usuals—weed, beer, stale pizza, socks, garbage needing to go out—was a less familiar aroma. Sweet but tangy, a warm-pineapple dough/batter whiff, like the Hawaiian kind of pizza they never ordered, or pineapple-upsidedown-cake, or sweet-and-sour something.

Had Jake gotten Chinese food, or what?

Chinese food sounded pretty good, actually. His stomach rumbled.

A quick poke through the kitchenette turned up no evidence of takeout or bakery, and certainly no leftovers.

And there was a note of…he wasn't sure…

It kind of did smell like sex.

He looked at Jake's closed door. They didn't have a signal worked out, no sock on the doorknob or whatever, so, no help there. A couple of shuffling trying-to-be-stealthy steps in that direction made it clear, though, that the sweet-and-sour-sex smell was a lot stronger over that way.

So, he really *did* have a girl over?

Okay, then.

As the neighbor had said, good for him and all, way to go Jake.

Some guys had all the luck.

Finding half a package of generic sandwich cookies in a top cupboard—he would've preferred pineapple-upsidedown-cake—Marty plunked himself into his gaming chair and started up *Hellslayer*. He'd been planning to just go right to bed after his crappy night, but, as tired as he was, now his goal was to wait a while, game a while, and see who emerged from Jake's room. Would it be walk of shame, or slut-strut?

He played on autopilot and mute, barely registering it as legions of undead and demon minions exploded in silent gooey bursts. Scythe-claws, stinger tails, gaping slavering maws of teeth, infernal weapons etched in banefire, another day another dollar another trail of diabolical destruction.

His eyes were beginning to glaze over and he was about to pack it in anyway when a greenish flicker at the edge of the screen caught his attention.

Glitch? No, a glowie he'd never noticed before, tucked way back in a gloomy cavern corner. Secret save point? Given what was coming up in the game, that could be handy. He strode his rugged manly avatar toward it to investigate, though on the lookout for triggering ambushes or nasty surprises.

It was a goblet, studded with emeralds and sapphires. Not a piece of gear, he saw as he selected to it, but an unnamed and unidentified artifact he recognized from nowhere in the game lore. *Hellslayer* was riddled with Easter eggs, though,

and the prospect of being first to boast-post in the forums...
Add to inventory? Y/N.
Y, duh!
Activate? Y/N
Marty shrugged and hit Y again. If it nuked him, well, he knew where the last save point was.

Instead, the camera angle drew back and panned around, and suddenly he was in the middle of a cut scene he'd never seen before. His avatar lifted the gleaming goblet in both hands. Rays of light beamed from the jewels, brightening into an aura. The cup's contents swirled like a quicksilver galaxy.

His avatar tipped the cup and drank. The screen went cloudy, diffuse, with billowing smoky whorls of blue and green, which became gauzy silken curtains stirring, a room awash in their sheer draperies, suspended sultan's-tent-like around an immense and ornate oval bed.

"Well, and here you are," murmured the decadent Mila Kunis voice of Llylth, the demon queen. "Here you are at last...I've been waiting...hoping you would...come."

***

The guys were not gonna fuckin' believe this.

Hell, Spence himself wasn't sure he fuckin' believed it, and he was the one it was happening to.

"I'm tellin' ya," his cousin Pete had said, loading the last of the delivery into the rear of his rattletrap truck. "The Harmon sisters, couple real bow-wows, sure enough, but damn, get a slug of this into them, and they will be all over you like rats on a chicken carcass."

Spence had of course taken this to be more of Pete's bullshit, and wasn't about to go getting his hopes or anything else up. He'd been offered twenty bucks to make the drive out to Harmon's Creek, and twenty bucks was twenty bucks.

Besides, there was something about doing a midnight moonshine run through the backwoods backroads that appealed to him. Felt like heritage. Felt like hillbillying it old-school. The still in Pete's barn, the clay jugs and mason jars; shit, all they needed was Pappy in a rocker on the porch with a corncob pipe and a hound dog at his feet.

Pappy, however, was inside watching videos of Japanese schoolgirls on his computer, hated hound dogs, and his pipe-smoking days were long in the past on account of the cancer and the hole in his neck.

Nor was the drive any sort of *Dukes of Hazzard* law-dodging yee-haw. No bumbling deputies, no evil revenuers, no raucous chases down dirt roads and jumping the crick when the bridge proved out. A little disappointing, though he doubted his cousin's truck could have taken much punishment, and the jugs of 'shine in the back surely couldn't.

That the Harmon sisters were in fact a couple real bow-wows proved without dispute. One tall and scrawny, scrawnier even than him, with hair like dried mop-strings; the other almost short enough to be a genuine dwarf, a stocky fireplug of a thing.

But they thought he looked "jist an ab-see-lute *ringer* for that crossbow-totin' dreamboat on that there zombie show, don't he?" and, well, an empty jar or so later…

So, here he was, sprawled with his pants around his ankles on the bare mattress of a swaybacked king-size, in a room with travel-agency posters tacked to the faux-wood paneling—sunny beaches, Florida, California, Hawaii—while both Harmon sisters totally went to town on him. Bow-wows, maybe, but could they ever suck a dick! One on either side of him, taking turns or working it together, sometimes pausing to kiss each other all sloppy-slobbery and open-mouthed before going back to slurping on his cockmeat like it was a honey-dipped corndog.

The moonshine ran warm through his bloodstream, and his brain felt steam-clouded. He made a token effort or two to fondle a tit—the scrawny sister was ironing-board flat but had big hard lug-nut nipples, while the dwarf-sister sported a firm round little softball set—and for the most part was content to lie there and let them have their fun. The 'shine took no detrimental toll on his performance; his first load pumped down the scrawny sister's throat within a minute, and twenty seconds later with the licking and nibbling continued unabated, he was rigid again, rarin' to go.

"You can thank me later," Pete had said.

Yes, indeed, Spencer certainly would!

Occasional worries crept into his brain... there might be trouble, there might be some angry hulking Harmon brothers around, or a scowling Big Daddy Harmon with a shotgun.

He knew the kinds of things that could happen out here, not far distance-wise but worlds away from fancy-ass Fairmont...had seen and even participated in them with his own family...when one of Jolene's boyfriends broke her arm and stole her car, Spence had been among the Bodeans who went and took care of it.

Luckily for him, no Harmon menfolk showed up.

Big Mama Harmon *did*.

The door swung open and there she was, filling the frame top-to-bottom and side-to-side, close on four hundred pounds of jiggling rolls in an aqua-blue mu-mu; what her daughters lacked in tits and ass, she *more* than made up for. The scent of toaster pastries—flakey-bakey crust, sweet frosting, and fruity filling—hung around her like fine perfume.

The king-sized creaked as she crawled herself onto it, bulling her daughters aside the way a walrus might push through a pack of seals. A moment later, she had Spence swallowed root-deep, while the other two tongued at his balls and butthole.

Pete had not mentioned this!

Thank him later? Spencer would send him a goddamn gift-basket!

Big Mama Harmon drew back at the last moment and he blew a gusher all over the naked mammoth mounds of her chest. She used his still-throbbing cock to smear the spunk around like warm and creamy fingerpaint, then titty-humped him hard again in that slippery valley while her greedy cumslut daughters lapped up the excess.

He may've blacked out there for a minute, from the sheer intensity. Didn't slow them or his dick down at all; when he

101

could again focus, it was to the most amazing yet sensations of suction and friction; he had never experienced or so much as imagined anything like it! Almost more than he could take!

Spence heard someone hollering and realized it was him, hollering himself hoarse, uttering every dirty word and blasphemy in his vocabulary, simultaneously begging for more and begging them to ease off a little before he ruptured something.

Lifting his head from the mattress took titanic effort. But he had to know which of them was doing this expert suck-work, this blowjob of the gods.

It wasn't Big Mama or either of her daughters. The face bobbing at his crotch belonged to some fuckin' relic, some hundred-year-old Harmon, all sagging skin like wrinkled linen, wisps of blue-white hair clinging to a paper-thin scalp.

Staring into those wide blind cataract-filmed eyes, weirdly greenish and seeming to glow, struck a horror-note memory, reminding Spence of some fucked-up story he had to read in school, something about a guy with one freaky-ass eye so the other guy chopped him up and buried him under the floor—

The crinkly lips, slick and shiny, parted in a dribbling grin. He saw sunken toothless gums, glistening-wet nubbed ridges of flesh, with his cock sliding between them as he helplessly kept thrusting into that ancient, lewdly slavering mouth.

INTERLUDE: VIGNETTES #4

Boys and their toys.

Junk-obsessed, and by no means is it only good ol' Sigmund Freud. Look at history, mythology, anthropology. Zeus, who couldn't keep it in his toga...Priapus, the god of colossal erections...Osiris had his cut off and fed to a croc, so that his widow Isis had to make a wooden one to conceive Horus...

As for Loki, well, even with the box-office success of a certain fourth-wall-breaking merc (shameless gimmick, that!), it's unlikely we're going to see Tom Hiddleston doing the bit where Loki ties his own scrotum to the beard of a goat.

The meat and veg, the wedding tackle, Mr. Happy and the Twins, call it what you will. The external male genitalia, to be more clinical.

But, if we're talking eunuchs—and we are now, because one was mentioned earlier, along with the dogfucker—it's more the lack or absence thereof.

Long-time lack or absence thereof. Not erectile dysfunction or late-in-life injury or gender reassignment surgery or the methods of chemical castration they sometimes try to use to treat sex offenders.

Eunuch-eunuch.

You might not think, in this day and age, there still are such things. Not in America, anyway. That's more for, like, harem guards, right? Arabian Nights and Sinbad movies. Those pudgy dudes in charge of making sure no other swinging dicks go messing around with the sultan's gardenful of wives, concubines, and olive-oil slave babes.

Doesn't happen *here*! Not here in the greatest nation, apex of the free and civilized world, 'Merica! Get real.

103

That's history and third-world shit, primitive, barbaric, right up there with ritual cannibalism and stoning people to death!

***

Uh-huh. Tell that to Enoch Shaw.

His parents were good Christians. That's what they believed, that's what they didn't just claim but *proclaimed.* Often.

Because God. Because Jesus. Because the Bible.

Because sin and sex and evil and temptation and Heaven and Hell.

Remember Carrie's mom and all those other religious whackadoo fanatics from Stephen King books? Ever seen those news articles about people who let their kids starve or suffer or die waiting for a miracle? The Lord will provide, though not in the form of, oh, say, medical intervention, vaccines, drugs, transplants and transfusions, no. Those are all sciencey and scary and therefore the Devil's work. Pray the gay away. Truss up your troublesome tweens in blankets to be 'reborn' and stop their backchatting.

That kind of thing is what we're going for here. That's how the ever-so-holy Shaws were. Better than you. Better than everyone else. Married in sacred abstinence, unpolluting of the flesh, above all those perverse and worldly lusts, yadda-yadda.

Golly-gee-whillikers what a surprise it was when she turned up preggers. Oops. Awkward. Embarrassing. To their credit, at least they didn't go so far as to try the Virgin Mary excuse. No angels or Holy Ghosts or acts of God presumptions.

Besides, by admitting their fall from grace, they could wallow in repentance, really get down and abject and mortificational with their sinful selves, wear the hair shirts, do the martyrdom mambo. And, best of all, they could make sure *their* child would be godly from the get-go. Their child would never give in to such wicked temptations.

Along comes Baby Enoch.

He might've been better off if they'd gone extreme anchorite—another word from ancient Greek, and another real actual historical thing people used to do; look at us, just learning stuff all over this shit!—and just walled him up inside a monastery, denied all human contact except for hearing the singing and the sermons. Maybe they couldn't find a bunch of monks who'd go for it. Who knows.

Instead, the proud parents celebrated not with cigars, but with a heavy-duty rubber band. Maybe a different sort of rubber would have saved the Shaws the problem in the first place, but just try telling them that.

Anyway. Ever stretch-twist-wrap a rubber band really tight around your finger? Interfering with your circulation, causing this cold, weird, numb, bloodless lump of alien-feeling meat?

Imagine someone doing that to a baby. A baby boy. Only, not to his finger. To his whole newborn package, inoffensive little grape-cluster though it may be.

And leaving it there.

You know what happens to the umbilical cord, after it's cut and tied? How the excess part sort of withers, atrophies, dries up, and falls off? And that's where belly-buttons come from?

Yeah. Like that. Pretty much like that.

***

Of course, some men have the exact opposite problem.

Rodney Edwards is one of them. He is hung like a horse. Packing serious pipe. His ballsack alone suggests he's smuggling eggplants. Flaccid, Dickzilla reaches halfway to his knees, and is, as they say, a grow-er as well as a show-er. At full attention, it's as if someone welded half a six-pack end to end.

His is, admittedly, a problem a lot guys might not think of *as* a problem, a problem most guys think they should be so lucky to have. They think, based on porn, it's what women want. So do some women, inexperienced enough with the real world not to know better.

Rodney knows better. He knows all too well how bottoming out against a cervix can be less than fun for both parties. He knows porn and reality often don't match. He knows what it's like to not have enough blood to run both ends of his body at the same time, and the trouble a raging hard-on can cause an otherwise sensible brain.

In many ways, he's a living, breathing stereotype and he knows that, too—a six-foot-ten slab of mahogany muscle with a voice to make panties spontaneously combust, the black man in whose presence white girls go giddy and white boys go 'whoa.'

The irony of his name hasn't been lost on him, either. Rodney, emphasis on *Rod*. Nor has his chosen profession. As a teenager, he heard and bought into the bullshit about locks and keys, how a good key could open any lock but only a cheap and easy lock opened for any key, and decided whatever else, he was gonna be one badass locksmith keymaster mofo.

Rodney racked up quite a list by the time he was old enough to buy a legal drink, including two baby-mamas. His third baby-mama became his first ex-wife, after the two of them and a couple of his girlfriends appeared on one of those trashy afternoon talk shows, at which point one of the girlfriends also dropped the bomb about becoming baby-mama number four.

Eventually, Rodney decided enough was about enough. He pulled his act together, relocated to a new part of the state, and vowed to keep it strictly casual from here on out. No strings, no muss, no fuss, no bother. Aside, of course, from the child support and occasional visits with some of his kids.

He owns his own business, Lock Steady. The walk-in trade is next to nothing, but out-calls and emergencies are where it's at. He gets a lot of those from well-to-do Fairmont ladies who misplace their keys on a regular basis, as well as tipsy wine-tasting tourists. The latter, if they treat him right, he'll refer to a friend with a local taxi service to save them the added hassle and expense of risking a ticket...and if they don't treat him right, he'll send word to another friend, one with the county sheriff's department. Both of which friends are usually inclined to appreciate the arrangement. These days, Rodney does all right. He's a little older, a little wiser, and has finally come to realize being invited over and welcomed in is the best way to go, far better than any amount of doorbusting force or lockpicking finesse.

It did raise some eyebrows around town when he hired a then-high-school girl to cover part-time hours at the shop, but he and Beth, they have an understanding.

Besides, she isn't his type.

***

Enoch, though?

Poor Enoch. All he has left down there is this shriveled nub of an outie, this raisin-sized skin-tag with a pee-hole. Which, he goes sitting down, by the way, and it's not the tidiest process. Less stream, and more sprinkler-spray.

No sensation, either. Not much in the way of testosterone or urges or anything of the sort.

His parents honestly expected this to make him grow up pure. Pure in body, mind, and soul. Pure in thought, act, and deed. Pure, holy, godly, saintly. Free from sin and temptation.

They expected he would, one day, thank them for their noble selflessness, their sacrifices on his behalf.

Needless to say, they were disappointed.

Or, would have been, if they'd lived long enough.

Not that he murdered them; don't go getting that kind of idea!

He tried to be the son they wanted, he really did. He went to church, and he followed their rules. His parents protected him, sheltered and shielded him. None of that sinfulness of television or public school for their son! None of those wicked doctors; if Enoch got a fever or a tummyache, it was God's will and he needed to be good and pray.

When he inevitably asked where babies came from, or

107

why some ladies who wanted babies didn't have them while some ladies had more babies than they could take care of, they told him that was also God's will. God's blessing or punishment, depending.

It wasn't until about age ten that the doubts began to seep in, and it began to occur to him he was in some fundamental way different from the other boys. He couldn't understand why some of his friends were starting to change—their voices, their bodies, their sudden interests in girls.

He thought everyone was like him, you know, 'down there.'

When the truth finally hit, it hit *hard*.

These days, of course, little Enoch is all grown up. He's successful in his career, well-to-do, happily married.

He has a lot of kids.

Four, with his wife. Okay, the oldest is adopted and the other three took some work, but, they're still his.

Them, and many more. Dozens more. Hundreds more.

You'd never know it to look at him. He's no Rodney; far from it. He's roundish and softish, smooth-skinned, pudgy-featured. On the phone, he's easily and often mistaken for one of his younger sons.

He's never had sex.

He's never wanted to.

The Shaws achieved that goal, at least.

Not only is it physically impossible, but he considers the biological processes of arousal and intercourse to be crude, disgusting. He regards the act with a clinical curiosity and revulsion.

But he is fascinated, even obsessed, with making babies.

CHAPTER THIRTEEN
SUSPICION

Lock Steady's storefront consisted of dulled-glass display cases and metal shelves stocked with padlocks, bike chains, hide-a-key gadgets, handcuffs, and lockboxes. A wire spinny-rack of novelty keychains sat on the counter, next to the cash register.

Beth, slouched on a high stool, ground out her cigarette butt in an ashtray atop a stack of industry hardware catalogs and order forms. Technically, the shop was no smoking, but Rodney gave zero shits as long as she showed up and did her job. Most of which was phone and computer out-calls anyway; she could hardly remember the last time an in-the-flesh customer had walked in.

When the door opened, jangling a cluster of old key-blanks instead of anything cutesy like a bell, she damn near fell off the duct-taped vinyl seat.

But it was only Devon.

Which, on its own, was still weird, and not just because none of her friends were much in the habit of dropping by. For one thing, it was a weekend evening, prime wine-trade tourist traffic time; his folks' bistro should have been bustling, with free slave labor all hands on deck.

For another, the guys had been flakier than usual for like days now. To the point she'd been starting to wonder if they were pissed at her about something…what, she couldn't guess…even if Jake was still embarrassed over the summoning clusterfuck, and the way they'd teased him about thinking his Nachtwald ancestry gave him super warlock powers or whatever, it didn't explain the others.

Then again, since when had Spencer or Marty needed an explanation for being flakey? As for Brendan, let him sulk, no great loss, she stood by her earlier to-hell-with-him.

And Devon…well, but, here he was.

"You look like shit," Beth said.

He did. Sallow, sweaty, eyes kind of sunken-starey, lips chapped and chewed. No wonder he was on the loose; his parents couldn't run any sort of restaurant with one of their servers going around like lukewarm plague-on-a-stick.

"Do I? Uh, yeah, I guess. Sorry."

"You sick or something? Don't breathe at me."

"I won't. I'm not. I just haven't been, uh, sleeping. Listen, Beth…"

She listened, raising an eyebrow to encourage him along, but he didn't follow up his 'Listen, Beth' by, you know, actually *saying* anything. He stood there, fidgeting, shifting his weight—of which he seemed to have lost some—from foot to foot.

"Yyyyeah?" she prompted.

"I wanted to apologize."

"Okay…"

"I mean, I was dumb…you've got every right to be mad at me for the way I acted, but…it surprised me, that's all, and…I freaked out, I panicked…so I wanted to apologize."

"Okay," she said again.

"…and, uh, to see if maybe you'd give me another chance."

"At what?"

Devon shuffled his feet some more, stirring the floor's dirty grit of dust and fine metal shavings from the key grinder. He stammer-mumbled something that might've included the word 'tattoo.'

"What?"

"Seeing your tattoo!" he blurted, turning red. "Another chance. I'd really like to. I think you're great, I just didn't think you thought I—"

"Whoa, whoa, *whoa!*" Beth went palms-out. "Back it up, new kid, back it *right* up. I don't know where you got the idea—"

"The other night! When we were walking back from Jake's!"

"Yeah, so?"

"And…and you…with the…" He flapped a hand toward her torso. "The…with your boobs, and asking did I want to see your tattoo, and I panicked, it was stupid, I freaked out and ran away, and you probably hate me but I didn't *mean* to offend you it wasn't like that at all, and oh *jeez* I'm such an asshole I'm really making a mess of this!"

She gaped at him. "*What* was that about my boobs? What are you talking about?"

"I'm sorry!" Devon wailed, grabbing the sides of his head as if it was going to explode. He spun in a clumsy one-eighty, knocking the wire keychain rack off the counter, and bolted for the door.

"Dev!" Beth sprang off the stool, knocking more stuff off the counter—the stack of catalogs and her ashtray—but he was already outside and running up the street.

The hell?

Plunking her butt back down, she stared incredulously at nothing in particular, trying to find some sense in the crazy. It didn't help. She messaged Jake, got no reply. Messaged Spence, same thing. Marty made it zero-for-three.

Flakes. A bunch of damn flakes.

She tried a couple of other Bodeans she had contact info for, but none of them knew where Spencer was. She tried calling Jake, and got voicemail. Finally, annoyed, she dialed the Shop-N-Go, past caring if it caused Marty trouble with his boss.

"He isn't *here*," said a woman named Gina, who sounded even more annoyed than Beth felt. "Called out sick last minute. Again! Twice this week, so *I'm* stuck doing a double, covering for his lazy slacker ass. Well, I'm telling you, he does it tomorrow, I will personally track him down and see to it he has to call in *dead*!"

"Hey, I hear you," Beth said.

"You know what I think?" Gina went on, building into a righteous froth. "I think he's parked in front of some video game!"

"Probably."

"If you find him, you let him know I am done putting up with his shit!"

"I will."

She hung up, and scowled at the phone. It wouldn't be the first time Marty blew off work for that kind of reason—the new Fallout, a midnight geek-movie premiere—but he usually mentioned it beforehand. Hell, he usually wouldn't shut up about it beforehand.

A check of the clock showed her she had forty-five minutes left on her shift.

Screw it. Close enough. This was bugging her, and it was going to continue to bug her, until she got some answers.

She punched in the codes to route any after-hours calls to Rodney's cell, closed up, locked up, and headed for Jake and Marty's building. Their windows were dark, absent even the usual flicker of TV screen or monitors. Beth tromped up the steps anyway, phone in hand and thumbs texting, hardly watching where she was going, and damn near tripped over Devon.

He was sitting with his back to the door, knees drawn up, arms around his shins, and when he recognized her, he flinched like he expected a smack in the face.

After whatever he'd said about her boobs, Beth *was* kinda tempted. And maybe it'd knock some sense into him; the new kid seemed to have gone a little off the rails. She held back, though, shoved her phone in her pocket, and gave him a narrow-eyed look.

"What are you doing here?" she asked.

Devon flinched again. "Nothing, I just…I, uh…wanted to talk to someone, but…nobody's home."

"So, you can talk to me," Beth said. "You can explain what the hell all that was, back at the shop."

"What all what was?" a familiar voice interrupted, as Spencer made his way up the stairs.

Beth peered at him. "What's with you? You're walking funny."

"No shit." He grinned a lewd, smirking, exhausted grin. "You are not gonna fuckin' believe it when I tell ya. I hardly fuckin' believe it myself, and I was there. But why the fuck's everybody hanging around outside?"

"Dev says nobody's home."

"Sure, Mart-O's at work, but Jake—"

"Mart-O's not at work." She relayed her conversation with Gina.

"Well then, he's gotta be here. Where the fuck else would he go?"

"That's what I figured."

"And why's the new kid acting like you're gonna feed him his own ass?"

"I might have to," she said, giving Devon another helping of the narrow-eyed look. "If he keeps cracking jokes about my boobs."

"Jokes? What? No! I didn't...I..."

"Okay, this I gotta hear, but, let's go inside first, huh? I'm fuckin' beat." Spence tried the knob, found it locked, then banged on the door. "Yo! Jake! Mart-O! It's us. Open up."

"Shh!" Devon hissed in warning, jerking his head toward the next apartment. Its windows were not totally dark; a faint bluish glimmer shone through a crack in the drapes.

They waited for a tense moment, but the big bald neighbor did not burst out and rearrange their teeth for them. All stayed quiet.

"Don't you have a key?" Beth asked. "You crash on their couch often enough."

"Kiddin' me? *Coach* won't trust me with a key to his place, and I'm his fuckin' nephew."

She blew an exasperated breath. "Fine. Move."

"What're you doing?" asked Devon, as she crouched and fiddled with her phone.

"Opening the damn door."

"There's an app for that?"

"You really *do* want me to feed you your ass, don't you?"

"Sorry..."

"I don't know what you did, bro," Spencer said, "but it must've been epic."

"I didn't do anything!"

He ignored that and bent over Beth's shoulder. "You keep lockpicks in your cell phone case?"

"I work for a damn locksmith, don't I?"

"Nice. The ol' B&E."

"No B," Beth said. The lock, a flimsy cheapo mickey-mouser she probably could have popped with a paperclip, let go. "Just E."

Spencer pushed, and the door swung inward onto the obstacle-course gloom of Jake and Marty's living room. The usual debris field of Mega Guzzle cups, chip bags, and snack-cake wrappers surrounded the gaming chair, but the chair itself was empty. So was the couch. Both bedroom doors were shut. The air was stale, funky, dank with old weed, and kind of foul...foul, with a weird hint of something that reminded her of those candles her mom liked, the cookie-and pie-scented ones.

"This doesn't seem right," Devon said.

"Enh, it's only kinda illegal," Spence said.

"That's not what I meant."

"Well, what did you mean, then?" asked Beth, rounding on him, fed up with the whole bunch of them but at least here was one she could take it out on. "What was all that stuff about my boobs and wanting to see my tattoo and everything?"

"Oh, this gonna be *gooood*," Spence said, flopping onto the couch. "When'd you get inked? Thought you were waiting 'til you could afford a pro, not that scuzzbag in Winston City."

"I didn't, and I am, so shut up."

Devon blinked, baffled. "You mean, you don't have a tattoo? You were...you were just messing with me? Was that just some kind of game? Jeez, Beth!"

"Was *what* some kind of game?"

"All that stuff about being hurt we didn't think of you as a girl, and how you had the most amazing boobs, and... and...and...hitting on me!"

She caught Spencer's agog expression of shocked delight out of the corner of her eye and resolved to deal with *him* later.

114

"Are you fucking insane?" she shouted at Devon. Then they were both shouting. Him bleating and protesting and digging himself in deeper by trying to reassure her that her boobs really *were* amazing and he'd only freaked out and run away because he was stupid; her getting more and more pissed and insisting she had done *no* such thing, *would* do no such thing, her boobs—amazing or not—were *none* of his goddamn business. With Spence watching like it was the greatest high-speed tennis match in history, whooping and cackling, downright *chortling*, the shit!

Into the middle of it stumbled Jake, Jake with total disheveled bed-head, one eye only half-open and the other sleep-puffed. Jake in nothing but a pair of boxers hanging halfway off his hips.

"Guys…hey…guys, seriously…keep it down, huh? What time is it? What's with the yelling?"

Marty emerged from his own room, scowling, badly in need of a shower and looking like he'd been wearing the same t-shirt and sweats for three days. "Dude. *You* should talk. Not as if you're fooling anybody."

"Huh?"

"Did you sneak her out the window again, or what?"

"Sneak who out the window?" Spence cut in.

"Cynthia-Lynne Abbott," Marty said.

Jake started, guilt waking his groggy expression right up. The others jawdropped and boggled.

"Look, I know about you and her, okay?" Marty continued. "You don't have to do this, hide it, lie about it, whatever."

Further chaos ensued, everybody talking at once, trying to talk over each other, Spencer demanding to know what the fuck he'd missed, Jake telling Marty it wasn't what he thought, Marty telling Jake oh it was but they were still cool right still bros right, Devon aghast that Jake could do that to his best friend I mean *jeez* they all knew how Marty felt about her, Marty claiming hey no he was good yeah okay maybe not thrilled and Jake damn well better treat her right not jerk her around like that asshole Troy-fucking-Cahill and anyway he didn't *need* Cynthia-Lynne Abbott anymore because he had someone *better*, and Spencer remarking it was like starting a show mid-season shit he hadn't been away *that* long had he but holy fuck you guys wait until they heard what *he'd* been doing, and Beth wanting to know what the hell was *with* everybody lately because she'd known they were all disgusting horndogs but this was getting crazy, and Devon protesting he *wasn't* a disgusting horndog honest he wasn't but if she still wanted to hook up give him another chance he liked her a lot and was super sorry he'd freaked out, and Beth outraging at him hook up yeah *right* in your *dreams*, and finally Jake—

"Guys! Shut up a second!"

Incredibly, they all did, and looked at him. He had both eyes open now, both eyes wide open, alight and aware.

"Dreams," he repeated. "What Beth said, in your dreams, in our dreams, it's our dreams...do you know what this means? We did it!"

CHAPTER FOURTEEN
CONFRONTATION

And the chaotic shouting following *that*, well…

Eventually, Jake got them all simmered down enough to have some sort of coherent conversation. With a break for him to put some clothes on. Kind of a challenge to be the leader and voice of reason in just his boxers.

But it made sense now.

It all made sense.

If he could just get the others to accept it.

To get past their indignation and disbelief.

And their guilt, mortification, embarrassment, and shame.

"So, you're saying," Beth said, "that you've all been having weird freaky sex dreams you thought were *real*?"

Her tone was beyond dangerous, all the way to lethal, and the *look* she sent Devon's direction made the new kid tuck in on himself like a turtle.

"No fuckin' way," Spencer said. "If I was gonna dream something like that, it'd be with cheerleaders and supermodels and shit, not a mother-daughters-granny fiveway with the Harmons. *No* fuckin' way."

"Look, one thing at a time," Jake said. "First off, Beth, you did *not* make any moves on Dev, right?"

"Are you *seriously* asking me—?"

"So, if you didn't, he *must've* dreamed it, right? We all did, we each did."

Marty cast a disconsolate glance at his gaming setup, as if the *Hellslayer* demon-queen really could have crawled out of the screen like the chick from *The Ring*. Then he brightened a bit, kind of a pitiful brightening. "Then, wait, so, Jake… you're not…you weren't…with Cynthia-Lynne…?"

Jake shook his head. "I hardly even know her, talked to her like maybe once since school. Even if she *was* checking

117

me out at the Green the other day, c'mon, I'm not Mister Super-Stud. Besides, like you said, bros, right?"

"But she did text me about you."

"Hey, maybe she did, I don't know, doesn't mean I've been banging her behind your back. If I was going to, I wouldn't bring her *here!*"

"No fuckin' way," repeated Spencer, as if to himself. "Porn stars or something, give me some fuckin' credit. Why *dream* a redneck fuck-fest?"

"If Jake's right, though..." Devon gulped and slid a nervous, semi-hopeful smile toward Beth. "Then it wasn't our fault, the stuff we...said and did. It doesn't count, it wasn't real."

"Doesn't count?" she echoed, and man it was withering. "Doesn't *count*? You fantasize *me, me* as a slut hitting on you, and somehow that's supposed to be *okay*?"

"Yeah, dude, you sex-dreamed about *Beth*? Sick."

"Drop dead, Marty!"

"Not to mention pussied out. Who pussies out in his own sex-dream? You want to argue against a for-real succubus scenario, there's—"

"You can drop dead too, Spencer!"

"The fuck is your problem, anyway?"

"I don't want to hear about your wank-fantasies, and I *sure* don't want to hear about them if they involve *me*; that's messed up, that's gross, nobody wants to hear that. 'Hey I thought about you while I was jerking it last night,' *not* cool, right up there with sending dick pics, who the hell thinks that's a good idea?"

"That's Dev, not me—"

"Him, you and your redneck fuck-fest, Marty and some video game bimbo, what's the difference? And now you want to say it was a succubus? The devil made you do it? That's pretty weak, right there."

"The succubus thing, that's *Jake*, not me—"

"Wasn't it your idea in the first place?" said Devon.

"Yeah, but I didn't believe it!"

"Why'd you suggest it, then?"

"Guys, c'mon, chill a minute," Jake said. "Just think about it. The ritual—"

"Was Brendan fuckin' with us, remember?"

"Anybody ever hear from him yet?" wondered Marty.

"No, and who the fuck cares?"

Jake paused, an odd cool sinking in his stomach. "Though, if we *did* summon something…here we've been figuring Brendan's staying away from us, but…"

"Oh for shit's sake!" Beth flung her hands in the air. "This is nuts."

"Maybe we should take a look at the video."

"Why?"

"Proof."

She barked a humorless laugh. "Of what? You say it worked? Okay, so, where is she, then, huh? Where's this sexy succubus of yours? Let's see her. Bring her on in!"

"Beth—"

"No, she's got a point," Spencer said. "You want proof, that'd be proof."

Nobody said anything. Jake looked at Marty, who looked back and him with a bewildered shrug. Only then, in the moment of silence, did it dawn on him again how much noise they'd been making, raised voices in the middle of the night, and how lucky they were the scary neighbor hadn't come crashing through the wall like the Kool-Aid Man. Bullet dodged, or they would've been well and truly hosed.

"Jeez, you guys," he said in a hoarse whisper. "We can't be doing this. Someone's going to call the cops on us or something. Guy next door's already got a hate-on at us. Good thing he must not be home."

"Looked like his TV was on when we came in," said Devon.

"Quit changing the subject." Beth stuck her fists on her hips and jutted her chin at Jake. "Where's your succubus, mister hot-shit wizard? Hiding it in your room? You and Marty been taking turns?"

Marty turned green. "Eew."

"Yeah, how would that be working, anyway?" Spence

asked. "Pass her around? Sloppy seconds, thirds, and fourths?"

"Not me, I didn't do—"

"Yeah, yeah, new kid, we know you didn't fuckin' do anything, you fuckin' pussied out."

"Drop it already, why don't you?" Beth said. "You're all a bunch of pervs."

"There's a news flash." Spence snorted.

"Know what? Okay. Whatever. I'm done." She started for the door.

"Beth, wait!" Jake almost set a hand on her shoulder, realized that would be a good way to spend part of his day in the E.R. with a broken wrist, and stopped. "Let's just watch the video, okay? Let's make sure."

"Watch it yourselves, do what you want, I don't care. Leave me out of it."

"You're not leaving because of—" Devon began.

"Don't even talk to me."

Then she was gone, slamming the door hard enough to topple a stack of DVD cases and make Marty's framed autographed Rooster Teeth poster rattle on the wall.

Spencer whistled low. "She is *piiiiissed*, never seen her so pissed."

"It's my fault," said Devon.

"Yep."

"Yeah."

"Fuckin' A."

"Should I go after—?"

"Dude, I wouldn't."

"Are you fuckin' nuts?"

"Better let her cool down," Jake said. "If you went after her right now, she'd rip your balls off and bounce them down the street."

Devon slumped in his seat, mumbling how it wasn't fair, he didn't mean to, he didn't know, he didn't even *do* anything anyway…Spencer told him hey cheer up at least it was a girl; here the rest of them had been wondering if he was a fagola or something; which was fine if he was but he could've said…Marty just went, "*Beth*?" again, as if that was going to help.

"Okay, guys, c'mon, listen," Jake said. "I think we're agreed on this much: they were dreams, right? We've all been having these weird—intense and hot, but, weird—dreams. Right?"

"Speak for yourself—ahhh, fuck, fine, fine, dreams, sure. But I'm tellin' ya, that fuckin' hick with his crossbow, he's a get-laid goldmine for the likes of me. I should get a motorcycle; I'd be chin-deep in va-jay-jay."

"Dude!"

"And it still doesn't prove jack shit about demons. Only proves what Beth said, we're a bunch of pervo jacker horndogs."

"This whole thing was your idea in the first place," Marty told him.

"Don't get me wrong, I still think it'd be fuckin' awesome, wish it *was* true we had us a real succubus sluttin' around. If it's dreams, though, where's the evidence?"

"What do you mean, evidence?" asked Devon.

"The fuck you think I mean? Tissues, sheets, the ol' crusty fucksock." He tossed his head swagger-like and did the *this*-guy thumbs. "I dunno for the rest of you, but the way *I* been feelin' lately? It's goin' *somewhere*."

Marty looked at Jake. Jake looked at Marty. Devon looked away, suddenly captivated or deeply concerned with something in the corner.

"That's…not a bad point, actually," Jake finally said. "I swear, I have not had any girls over, let alone what's-her-name, and…"

"And we all know *I* haven't," said Marty, not without bitterness. "So then…"

"Maybe we really *should* watch the video," Jake said. "Just to make sure."

They watched the video.

They made sure.

"Oh, shit," somebody whispered.

Everything Jake had been trying really hard not to think

121

about, to not remember…everything he'd been repressing and forcing violently from his mind…

It had been easy, so easy, to give in and go along, to let himself accept the illusion believe the seductive lies immerse and ignore…ignore the truth, ignore the reality…

Go with it like a drug, a buzz, a rush…ride the wave… hypnotic and hallucinogenic…the sensation and pleasure and ecstasy…

"What *is* it?" Devon sounded queasy.

"*Not* a sexy demon chick," said Marty.

"But it *is* what we summoned," Jake said. "The ritual worked. It really did."

They watched the video again. And again. Full screen. Pausing it. Frame-by-frame. Until there could be no doubt of what they were seeing, no debunking, however much they might have wanted to.

The way it moved…the way it squished and squelched… its gelatinous, sea-slug, quivering *aliveness*…the bioluminescent pulsating blue-green glow and the memory of how it had *smelled*, how it had *felt*…

"That's what we been stickin' our dicks in," Spencer said.

And if it had been chaos before, what followed was screaming balls-to-the-wall pandemonium.

CHAPTER FIFTEEN
DISCUSSION

Beer and weed was probably a bad idea. But, as Spencer said, after that? They fuckin' needed it!

If not something even stronger.

Hard drugs and brain bleach came to mind.

With those not available, beer and weed would have to do.

Supplemented, in Marty's case at least, with some snackage. Salt, grease, sugar.

They'd each compared more extensive notes. Humiliating as it was to have to admit the details about his salacious encounters with Llylth and her host of succubus handmaidens—particularly the part how, for most of it, Marty wasn't himself-as-himself but his *Hellslayer* avatar; how lame could you get, not only fantasizing about being with someone else but about *being* someone else—he took some small solace in the fact that each of the others' stories were just as bad. If not worse.

Devon's Beth-thing, for instance.

Or Spencer, dreaming up his backwoods orgies.

He took considerably greater solace knowing at least Jake hadn't really been doing it with Cynthia-Lynne Abbott. She did deserve better than Troy-fucking-Cahill, yeah...but all the same...

"So," said Spence, releasing a long cloud of smoke. "The fuck do we *do*?"

"You agree it's a succubus?" Jake asked.

"I agree it's *some*-fuckin'-weirdass-critter, though you oughta sue the shit outta whoever wrote those spells. Talk about false-fuckin'-advertising."

"Well, we have to find it, don't we?" Devon said. "Find it and...banish it."

Jake popped another beer. "Yeah, I guess."

"Well I mean, you can't be thinking to…uh…keep it around."

"The ritual worked. We summoned it. That's pretty damn amazing, don't you think?"

"And we did say we wanted our own demon love-slave," added Spencer.

"A hot sexy naked devil-chick," Marty said. "Not a… jello-glob slug monster."

"Hey, you *got* hot sexy naked devil-chicks. Dunno what the fuck you're gripin' about."

"Look," said Jake, "they're supposed to be shape-shifters, right? Psychic. They read your mind and take on whatever form you most desire—"

"Call fuckin' shenanigans on that," Spence muttered.

"Dude, bright side…you could've got Beth, like Dev did."

Devon went bright red. "I didn't—"

"—*do* anything," they all finished for him.

"Shouldn't trash-talk Beth, anyway," Jake said. "She's our friend."

"Is it better I imagine she's shoving her boobs at me?"

"Hey!" squeaked Devon.

"How were they?" Spencer asked, then caught Jake's glare as Devon went from bright red to purple. "What? Pardon the fuck outta me for bein' curious."

"Can we focus, here, huh, guys? Spence is right, we do need to figure out what we're going to do about this. Whether we banish her or not—"

"*Her?*" echoed Marty.

"You prefer 'it'?"

"Good point."

"So, whether we banish her or not, we did summon her. That makes it our responsibility—"

"If we summoned her and she's our demon love-slave and all," Spencer said, "then where the fuck's she at? Shouldn't she be here? Or do we gotta be asleep, or what?"

"Yeah, how does it work? What are the rules?" Marty grimaced a little. "How do we decide, you know, whose turn it is?"

"What?" cried Devon. "You can't really be thinking about *keeping* her!"

"Wouldn't be sayin' that if you'd gone through with it instead of pussied out," said Spencer. "Okay, so we stuck our dicks in a blob-monster, but holy-fuckin'-*shit...*"

"Was it really that good?"

Marty nodded emphatically despite himself, and saw Jake doing the same. As horrible as it was, as horrible as he *knew* it was, as sick and wrong and gross and awful...that warm oozing jellyfish flesh touching him...sliming wetly over his skin...sure, in his mind it had been Llylth, her full lips hot mouth supple tongue deep throat...

Jeez, he didn't know how it was possible, drained and achy as he felt, but there he went with the start of another awkward boner. How was he ever going to make it back to work at this rate? Not like he could jump into the employee bathroom at the Shop-N-Go every ten minutes!

"Whether we keep her or what," Jake said, "we can worry about that later. First, we need to figure out how to control her—"

"Uh...you guys...I just thought of something." Devon either missed the look Jake gave him for interrupting, or didn't care. "You know how all this time we've been figuring Brendan was avoiding us, upset because nobody fell for his prank?"

Spencer scoffed like he was about to say something sarcastic, then choked on it. Marty froze with a handful of chips halfway raised. Jake's scowl did a sort of slow-motion dissolve into a gape of dawning comprehension.

They turned, as one, toward the screen. The video had ended on a blurred and askew image of grass, shadows, looming figures and haggard faces—the Shelter Park bums who'd come over to see what the commotion was, when the five of them made their crazy stampede exodus from Vault 420.

The five of them, because Brendan hadn't been with the group.

And they hadn't heard from him, he hadn't shown up or texted or anything, since.

Good riddance, hadn't that pretty much been the consensus? Guy's a douche, that stunt wasn't funny, fuck him the fuckin' fuckstick. Good-goddamn-riddance.

Except...

"Fuck," said Spencer, summing it succinctly.

Jake, meanwhile, grabbed his phone. There was no immediate reply, which, okay, well, it *was* the middle of the night, but all the same...

"If he's, um, missing, wouldn't someone have said?" asked Devon. "I know he doesn't have a job, but, what about his parents? He lives at home, right?"

"Sort of," Marty said. "Apartment over the garage, supposed to be for a housekeeper, but they gave it to him as a graduation present. Rent-free until he's twenty-five, the lucky bastard."

"So, they might not even know if he's gone?"

"Might not even notice. The way he talks, it sounds like his mom and dad are all work-work-work."

"He wasn't there when I went back down for the candlesticks and stuff," Jake said.

"But neither was Cumslut," said Spence. Seeing their reactions, he shrugged. "What? Why not fuckin' name her?"

"Cumslut?" Marty shook his head. "Dude."

"Not classy enough for ya?" He leaned back, puffed, and pondered. "How about Jizzabel?"

"Dude."

"Fellatrix," Jake suggested, grinning.

Devon put his hands over his eyes. "This is insane. Shouldn't we be—"

"Yeah." Jake stopped grinning, put on a sober expression, and struck a purposeful pose. "Yeah, we need to take care of this. It's our responsibility. Brendan may be a douche, but he *is* our friend, and since he wasn't pulling a prank on us, we owe it to him to find out what the hell happened. Save his butt, if it needs saving. Are you with me?"

As those big inspirational/motivational leader-speeches went, Marty had heard better in video game cut scenes. He got up anyway, brushing chip-crumbs from his chin and shirt, and crammed his last few snack-cakes and a can of generic soda into his jacket pockets.

Spencer and Devon followed similar suit, though, like Jake's speech, it was one of the weakest equipping montages Marty could recall. Tying shoes and grabbing phones was hardly buckling on armor, gear, and weapons.

Then again, they weren't going into battle, for crying out loud. No gangstas, no zombies, no mutated dire-rats or war-wolves. A few skeevy hobos at the park was about the worst of it.

"I see that fuckwad Tater again, he better keep his fuckin' crazy-ass yap shut," Spencer said. "Sayin' that shit about my ma..."

True shit, Marty knew, but you had to commend the Bodeans for familial loyalty. Marty's own parents had moved to one of those 55+ high desert condo communities; they made dutiful noises about visiting, but there was always a bridge tournament or casino field trip weekend or last minute doctor's appointment. They sent him the occasional card, usually with a check for fifty bucks and a note about how proud they were of him being so independent.

Subtle.

Still, an improvement on Jake's mother, who'd 'taken a break' to pursue her singing career when he was nine and never got around to coming back. His dad was a decent enough dude, for an absent-minded inventor type who forgot little things like, oh, say, eating or paying the electric bill. Fortunately for them both, there'd been Jake's grandparents in the picture.

Equipping montage over, they headed out, making the habitual effort to be quiet on the walkway and stairs. Though if the neighbor who'd complained about the noisy sex parties hadn't heard the earlier shouting, they were probably in the clear.

Not that 'probably in the clear' stopped Marty and Jake from sneaking surreptitious peeks at the windows. Dark, not a sound, not a sign of activity.

Same could be said for the street, and indeed most of

Fairmont, this late. Over in the fancy wine-snob part of town, some of the bars would still be open, and the hotel lounges, and ballrooms-slash-banquet-halls where any wedding receptions were going on.

Cynthia-Lynne Abbott would be over there somewhere. Marty hadn't been able to bring himself to message her, but now that he knew she wasn't seeing Jake…though what if she'd gone back to Troy again? She'd said she wouldn't, she'd said their break-up was for keeps this time, but she'd said that before. A lot. Almost as often as she'd said how hard it was to meet decent guys who weren't total assholes.

"Retards in a horror movie, Take 2," Spencer said as they neared the ominous black silence of Shelter Park. "Action."

"Ha, ha," said Devon.

There weren't even any bumfires burning in the homeless camp behind the low half-ring of bleachers. Tents and shacks sagged in the gloom, looking more derelict than ever. Derelict and depressing.

"Bet they're downtown, spare-changing," Jake said when Marty mentioned it, only half paying attention because of something over on the far side of the playground. "Hey… guys…that's not Brendan's car, is it? Under those trees?"

It was, parked where he'd left it the night of the ritual. Judging by the layer of leaves on its roof and hood, and the ticket tucked under a windshield wiper, it had been there ever since.

"Was it there when you came back?" Devon asked.

"I didn't notice. But…shit…shit, this isn't good."

"He must still be down there," Marty said. "What if he's hurt, or—"

"Don't fuckin' say it."

"C'mon." Jake strode toward the restrooms.

Marty hesitated. "I dunno, dude."

"We ran. We abandoned him."

"We thought he was yankin' our cranks!"

"Now we know better."

Dev took a deep breath. "Yeah. Yeah, okay. Yeah."

"Fuck," Spence said. "Fine, let's go, let's do this shit."

INTERLUDE: VIGNETTES #5

Unsurprisingly, the guys are about to go and get themselves into a bunch more trouble. Not like we couldn't see it coming; not like we didn't see it coming back in the prologue at the very start of the book.

It's about to get worse for them, but, let's throw in some more nasty gratuitous dogfucking and creepy-rapey first!

***

It's late, but the lateness of the hour doesn't make much difference to Lewis Bodean. Weekend, and not like he has a job to go to anyway. He managed to save up a tidy sum during his stint at Fairmont High, knows better than to lend money to his shiftless kin, and the only bitch he's got to support—besides his taxes going to welfare cases squeezing out one brat after another—is his good ol' Roxie.

He's settled comfortably in front of the TV, watching one of those movies with a title like *Spring Break Bikini Bimbo Beach Slaughter Bloodbath*. Even skimpier on plot than it is on costuming, and that suits Coach just fine. Sun, sand, surf, tits, ass, and a couple hundred gallons of corn syrup and food coloring.

Quality entertainment.

Coach cracks a fresh beer and pauses to lift it in a silent another-man-down tribute to a buddy of his who'd just announced his engagement earlier that day.

"Poor dumbfuck bastard."

True to form, the gal in question was closing in on the big 3-0, and wanted to lock herself down a meal ticket before time ran out. She'd had her fun, hopping in and out of beds, and would be happy enough now to dole out a semi-regular sex-ration to keep set for the rest of her life.

Hell, if she wasn't already knocked up, Coach was sure she'd see to it soon, just to further seal the deal.

During the next round of commercials, not needing to see more ads for barely-there rubbers, flavored vodka (Jesus wept!), or boner pills, Coach goes to zap some leftover chili and cornbread his sister had sent over. While it rotates in the microwave, he glances across to the Vilstreets' kitchen window, where the light's on.

And sure enough, talk about men being played for suckers and strung along, there's Hank Vilstreet at the sink, doing the dishes again. While Carla's no doubt upstairs in bed, nursing one of her 'migraines.'

How long, he wonders, until Hank has finally had enough?

You simply couldn't talk sense to the man. Lord knows Coach has tried.

Why, only yesterday, Carla had gone for one of her shopping trips and oh whoopsie-daisy when she got home she locked her keys in the car for what had to be the fourth time that month. Had to have the locksmith out to jimmy her inner workings with his big long tool…and open the car for her too.

Some deluxe service, all right. And to think, Hank will be getting the bill for that emergency call.

He takes his food back to his chair, right as the movie comes back with the Bikini Bimbos getting ready for the big wet t-shirt contest while the psycho with the dive-knives and speargun creeps closer to the couple skinny-dipping in the turquoise-clear lagoon.

Roxie abandons her gangly-legged sprawl in the other recliner and drapes her big head over his chair's arm, doing the soulful eyes routine.

"Even you have your wiles, don't you, girl?" He scratches behind her floppy ears and gives her half the cornbread. "No chili for you, though. My own are bad enough, and if *you* get going, it'll gas us out of house and home."

Her tail thumps his leg as she sloppily hoovers up the

crumbs. Then she's back, pushing her muzzle under his hand. Into his lap. Whining a little, nudging with her nose at his crotch.

Coach moves aside his bowl of chili and looks down, rather nonplussed. Yet, sure enough, she is nosing at his crotch, chuffing, rubbing her loose drooly jowls against his thigh. Wagging the tail. Doing more of the soulful eyes, all pleading, reflecting a blue-green shimmer from the TV where the skinny-dipping beauty is playing cocktease hide-and-seek with no idea her boyfriend's already skewered to a sunken log trying to struggle free before he drowns.

"Roxie?" he says.

She dog-grins at him, tongue lolling long and pink in that soft-meaty way, just running with slobber, puddling and soaking warm through his pants. Her normally foul dog-breath smells of cornbread, butter, and honey.

"Whatcha want, girl?" he asks.

He knows what it *seems* like she wants, but she has never done the likes of this before and he isn't quite sure how to react. Oh, she's obedient, she'll comply when he summons her up onto the bed and maneuvers her into position…she won't fuss or fight as he fucks her…confused, if anything, confused but cooperative because he's the man-master and she's the faithful bitch who'll do as she's told…and when he's done, when he's pumped his load, she'll go off to the corner to clean herself…

It's never occurred to him she might be liking it. That she might enjoy the feel of his cock sliding in and out, or the taste of his spunk as she lapped it up after.

More likely, she understands in her doggy way that *he* likes it, and she just wants to please him. Because he *is* the man-master and she's the faithful bitch.

And she is definitely nosing and nuzzling at his crotch— which is bulging and tented. Definitely dragging her long slobbery tongue along the fabric of his pants, whimpering as if begging for a treat.

Coach has heard the jokes about smearing peanut butter on your dick, and it'd be a lie to say he hasn't been tempted now and then, but he's also heard the jokes about some fellow who tries it only to get bitten...or find a hell of a moment to discover he's got an allergy.

Roxie, though, Roxie would never bite him. Certainly not on purpose, and he was willing to bet, not on accident.

Was he willing to bet?

Willing to bet his junk?

He eased her head out of his lap, leaned forward enough to put his beer and bowl of chili on the table, and then undid his belt. Her floppy ears perked at the sound. She sat back, attentive, tongue still lolling, dripping drool.

"Good girl. Gooooood Roxie. Yeah, there's my good girl, is this what you want?" Coach asked as he opened his fly and freed his rising interest.

She whuffed and panted, wagging.

"You be nice, now, you be a good girl, you mind those teeth, won't you?"

Then it was cold wet nose and warm wet tongue, licking and lapping and slurping, all up and down the shaft, around the head, nutsack and balls, and Coach sprawled back in his recliner, stifling a shout.

"Jesus God Mary and Joseph!"

And the slobbering drool, running, flowing, bathing him in dogslobber, as Roxie went to *town* on him dear *God* felt like that broad long supple tongue of hers wrapped him *completely*; pig in a blanket, enfolded, surrounded, engulfed, working him, milking him, bringing him to the brink so fast he can barely catch his breath.

"Oh, oh, oh yeah!" Panting himself now, gripping the arms of the recliner for all he's worth. "Oh, yeah, here it is! *Goooood* girl! Hnnnngh!"

He lets loose, comes like someone just struck oil, the dizzying spin-rush in his head so intense he realizes he's about to pass out...and the last he sees before he does is the glimmering lagoon-blue reflections in Roxie's eyes as she swallows down the torrent in great chug-a-lug gulps.

***

Meanwhile, across town, Troy Cahill has decided enough is enough.

He's tired of her games, tired of being played with. Oh, Cynthia-Lynne will do lots of things with him, will let him do lots of things to her, and will do lots of things to him...

Except for one thing.

Except for *the* one thing that counts, the main event, the real deal.

It isn't like he can't get it elsewhere. There are plenty of girls who are happy to. A lot of them right here in Fairmont. Several of them, supposedly Cynthia-Lynne's best friends.

It's the *principle*, damn it.

They've been dating, pretty seriously, on and off now, for years! He's taken her places, on trips, to concerts. He's bought her more dinners and presents than he can remember.

She owes him.

She fucking owes him, and she owes him fucking.

All her talk about waiting...for what? For a wedding night? For an engagement ring? Maybe their grandmothers had that why-buy-the-cow saying, but this is a world where you take it for a test drive before signing the papers.

As for saving it, there's a laugh. He's supposed to believe she's a virgin? He knows she's messed around with other guys, usually to try and make him jealous or get back at him for something. *He's* the one she wants to marry, so *he's* the one she'll hold out on, until she has that guaranteed commitment.

Hell, for all he knows, she and that hot-shit uncle of hers...

The more he thinks about it, the more he's convinced. Troy has never been a fan of Sebastian Abbott—rich, good-looking, arrogant, sleazy charm, a revolving door on his bedroom. Some of his conquests haven't been that much older than Cynthia-Lynne. Some of Troy's own conquests, Cynthia-Lynne's so-called best friends, have made no secret of the fact they'd drop their panties for Sebastian Abbott in a heartbeat.

And Cynthia-Lynne did have to learn her techniques somewhere. Why not at home? She'd known her way around handjobs and blowjobs long before Troy had the opportunity to offer any instruction.

So, yeah. The likelihood she's kept her V-card intact all this time, especially as much of a slut as she can be— she's always after him to rub her off or eat her out, always impatient, telling him he's doing it wrong—is, he figures, minimal.

Anyway, she owes him.

She owes him, and tonight is the night.

They've made up again, Troy having apologizing for whatever she was upset about this time. He's groveled and promised and even brought her a goddamn bouquet and a giant lemon cookie from her favorite bakery.

The make-up make-out turns nice and steamy, and for a few minutes there it almost seems a done deal. He has her down to her silky blue panties, which are filmy, almost transparent, almost not there at all.

But then she hits the brakes. Doing it in her usual cute-winsome way, where she twines her arms around his neck and kisses him and tells him it's great they're able to move past these silly little disagreements. And she's really glad he respects her wishes.

Was that when he decided enough was enough?

Was it a conscious decision, not only to get her drunk, but add a little something extra to her glass?

Not a problem, he says. He totally understands. They can put their clothes back on, maybe watch a few episodes of something, cuddle.

Whenever he decides, whether it's conscious or not, what matters is, it works.

Cynthia-Lynne is zonked.

Just totally zonked.

Troy doesn't waste any more time. He has to be careful; he doesn't want her to catch him. He doesn't want her to know, doesn't want her to be sure even if she suspects. Which means he can't come in her. He'll have to pull out. That's too bad, but at least he'll finally be fucking her.

She doesn't move as he pushes her skirt to her waist, as he takes off those silky-blue barely-there panties. Underneath, she is smooth as can be, nice and tidy, not a pube in sight.

Anticipating this?

Or, if not for him, then for whom?

He arranges her crossways on the bed with her legs— those long, holy-Judas-whoa legs—spread wide and dangling over the side. It's a high bed; with him standing, they're at the perfect accessible angle and height.

Troy may not want her to know for sure, but he also wants proof. He grabs his phone and takes a few quick extreme-close-up selfies. His hard-on, poised and ready between her thighs. His free hand popping a thumbs-up beside his hard-on. Another as he eases the tip in, finding the way warm, wet, and loose.

Halfway. Another pic. And deeper, balls-deep, all the way. Her insides are quivering, spasming, clasping at his cock. Pic. No denying it. He's in her, doing it for real.

Zonked? Or pretending to be, another of her games to see how far he'd go and getting more than she bargained for… and loving it…playing possum but giving herself away…

He withdraws almost entirely, takes one more pic to capture the sheen of juices, then sinks back in with a low, moaning sigh. As he starts the fucking in earnest, knowing he won't be able to last much longer, he darts a quick look at his phone just to make sure he's got—

What he sees makes him drop the phone. The screen stars and fractures in a spiderwebbed, useless crack-glaze.

But Troy doesn't notice, because the same thing is happening to his mind.

CHAPTER SIXTEEN
INVESTIGATION

Jake led the way, using his phone as a flashlight. The others followed crowded as close together as egos would allow—even if they would have rather been clutching each other like toddlers scared of the boogeyman, nobody wanted to be called a pussy.

The empty men's room felt colder, the echoes of their footsteps and breathing louder, the darkness more complete despite the phone-glows. Someone stepped on a paper bag with a bottle in it; the glass broke with a crack like a gunshot. The eye-watering fumes of cheap booze rose around them in a cloud.

Brendan, Jesus, they had left him behind. What about "no man left behind"? When they'd gone and *done* it?

But, Jake reminded himself, they hadn't known. They couldn't have known.

Now they were going to make it right.

Through the grout-crumbling hole in the tile-covered wall...into the stairwell...down the faintly rusty-smelling flights of metal stairs...to the underground network of hallways and bunkers...where, now, *none* of the wire-caged yellowed old lightbulbs seemed to be functioning.

Vault 420 was pretty much as he'd left it after his quick clean-up trip. The stuff he hadn't brought back out, he'd kicked into the corner so it was like any old pile of random trash. The lingering markings on the floor, burnt there in salt and soot, he'd scuffed to indistinguishable smudges. Anybody poking around would be able to tell something had gone on in here, but certainly not what.

"He's not here," Devon said, and winced as they shot him no-shit-Sherlock looks.

They passed several doors marked with stenciled number-letter combinations that reminded Jake of prison movie cell blocks. Some were long narrow rooms set up like dorms or barracks, with cots and bare bedframes. Others were identified as washrooms or storage closets.

Elsewhere down here, he knew, were larger spaces originally designed to serve as kitchens, cafeterias, gyms, med bays, and meeting halls. Enough to sustain several hundred people for months, if not years.

It must have been quite the ambitious project, back in the day. When Fairmont had been your typical wholesome American town, good patriots with faith in their government, all work ethics and family values, when kids still recited the Pledge of Allegiance in school, and the idea of anybody objecting to the 'under God' part would have been downright absurd.

They came to an intersection, their choices to the right and left wider and broader, while the one straight ahead continued narrow and darker than ever.

…but, from somewhere far down it, there came a rippling blue-green radiance like sunshine dazzling and dappling on tropical seas…

…and instead of the dank odors of mildew, rust, and stale piss…

…wafted delicate, enticing aromas…

…like funnel cake, fresh from the fryer, with sweet-fruity topping, and a generous mound of melting whipped cream…

…or rum drinks on a golden-sand beach, rum drinks with mango and pineapple and honey…

…vacations to places where they let you swim with the dolphins as the sea swelled and laved bathwater warm mild clear turquoise and the bone-white sand slipped tickling between your toes…

…girls in skimpy swimsuits, gauzy dresses, going topless…

…and he could almost smell the clean salt air, almost feel sun on bare skin and hear gentle breezes stirring delicate fronds…

…the aquamarine gleam and shimmer, weightless, fluid, water-ballet…

...a soft, low, throaty, purr of a laugh...

Not laughing *at* them, not a cruel mocking mean laugh, but a welcoming and inviting feminine chuckle...the kind that would be accompanied by the sly-slow come-hither of heavy-lidded long-lashed eyes...by the rich curve of a smile, and the glide of licked lips...

"It's *her*," Marty sighed.

"Aw yeah," said Spencer.

Devon faltered, blinking. "Maybe we—"

"Gonna pussy out again, new kid?"

"I...well..."

Jake thought of what they'd seen on the video, what they'd seen when Brendan lifted the dog dish and the wet, squelchy, glistening creature squirted from under it.

The gelatinous, quivering, loose-wrinkled skin-sack deflated balloon shape...the squirming feelers and polyps and writhing wormy tendrils...the shiny, bulging, grapelike clusters...flaps and folds peeling open with moist, fleshy sounds...orifices parting, puckering, gaping...hellish, hideous...

Their succubus.

Thanks to the ritual.

Thanks to him and his notions that having a distant drop of Nachtwald ancestry made him special, made him magic. Made him different and interesting, someone important.

Someone whose father would have paid attention to him, whose mother wouldn't have been too bored to stick around. Whose grandfather would be pleased that Jake had listened, and lived up to their heritage.

Actually, upon further consideration, maybe he'd gone about it a little wrong. Magic, okay. Arcane studies and occult lore, sure.

Summoning a sex-demon because he and his friends were pervy horndogs...

Yeah, probably less likely to make the family proud.

Even the Nachtwalds who'd cast hexes and death-spells on the neighbors might not really approve.

Well, something about it had worked, anyway. He didn't

know how special and important it made him, but, you had to admit, it was pretty different.

"C'mon," Jake said.

"You want to go closer?" asked Devon.

"We came down here to find her, didn't we?"

"I thought we came down here to find Brendan!"

"That, too."

Spence and Marty didn't contribute to that part of the conversation. They gazed at the blue-green glimmering flicker like they were half-hypnotized already...and maybe they were...maybe that was what she did...some combination of pheromones and telepathy...enticing them, tempting them...even though they knew...

Jake found his own feet had carried him several more steps down the corridor. Toward the light. Toward the scent. Toward the seductive promise of *her*, with his dick straining at his pants as if pointing the way, his own personal dowsing rod.

Pheromones and telepathy.

And demon powers.

Why else would he still be reacting this way, despite knowing what his logical, rational mind knew?

Why else would he want her?

Now that he knew, now that he did know, would it be different? What form would she take? Psychic shape-shifter, sexual chameleon, could he choose? If he concentrated on, say, Scarlett Johansson or Jennifer Lawrence...

"Wait here a second, you guys," he said.

"The fuck you mean, wait?"

"Dude, no fair! I got dibs."

"The fuck *you* got dibs? Nobody called fuckin' dibs."

"I'm calling them, then!"

"No dibs," Jake said. "We're not in third grade anymore. I just want to try something."

"Yeah, no shit," Spencer said. "Don't we all!"

"Wait here." He stabbed a finger at the floor.

"Who made you the boss?" Marty sulked.

"Um, shouldn't we be looking for Brendan—?"

"That's what I'm doing. I want to try talking to her."

If she just happened to look like Scar-Jo or J-Law while he was, well, hey, he had no problem with that. But it had to be him first, him alone, so she wasn't getting her signals crossed. God knew what she'd pick up from the whole group of them together; he didn't want to see some nightmare mash-up with elements from each.

He doubted they'd be able to wait there very long, if at all, so he hurried along the dark corridor with his phone angled to keep him from tripping over unseen obstacles on the floor.

Such as that blocky plastic kids' flashlight, where had *that* come from? He nudged it with his toe, turning it enough to see its dorky cartoon-character train-face, with its blank stare of dark dead-battery emptiness.

Creepy.

Jake stepped over it, avoided the ratty crumple of some discarded old coat—moldy, filthy, probably crawling with lice—and then the glow from his phone glinted on metal. The ridged edge of a key, a car key attached to a remote entry fob. With a couple of other keys on the ring.

Brendan's?

Almost had to be.

He shook them off and put them in his pocket. From behind came impatient mutters and mumbles—the fuck's takin' so long?

From ahead…

…the warm-cool blue-green…

…the sweet, doughy smell…that one kind of bread, those rolls…what was it called?…King's Hawaiian, yeah…he had loved that stuff when he was a kid. For picnics and parties and special occasions, fancier than ordinary drab dinner rolls, or a big entire single soft round loaf in an aluminum pan, pull it apart, eat it plain or slather it with butter…

…on a balmy, lazy, turquoise summer day out in the yard under the patio shade in the tickling grass the tickling and caressing grass, grass against his knees elbows tummy as he relaxed on the lawn…

…and she was so pretty he loved her so much loved her more than anyone her voice her laugh her perfume and shampoo and from where she was sitting he could see right up her skirt all the way up her skirt and she didn't know didn't know had no idea what he could see...

…funny feelings in his tummy, and lower, funny feelings feeling even funnier when he kind of wiggled and bounced his bottom…

…when she shifted when she moved when she crossed and uncrossed her legs the most beautiful lady in the whole wide world and he was going to marry her when he grew up…

Grown up, grown up yes, such a fine young man, so handsome, so healthy, so virile, so strong.

"What the hell, man? What is he doing?"

"He ain't whippin' it out again, is he?"

"Uh..."

Offer yes offer offer and give, your love your desire your pleasure your need our need our hunger feed and give.

…as beautiful as ever more beautiful than ever awash in a shimmering aura of liquid light reaching for him beckoning to him here with him again finally here to stay stay forever this time not leave never leave…

Come to us come to us come be with come be one all are we all are one come to be one with us into embrace engulf envelop and enfold be immersed be absorbed be as we be as one.

"Jake! Dude!"

"Aw shit!"

"Grab him!"

Sudden grabbing and grappling. Pulling at him. Yanking at him.

Shouting and swearing.

"Do you fuckin' *see* that?"

"Oh jeez oh jeez!"

Shaking him. Snapping him back to his senses.

Jake uttered a kind of ragged shriek-gasp.

For a terrible instant, he felt himself teetering as if on the edge of some ungodly precipice.

Then, looking down, he saw that he *was* on the edge of some ungodly precipice.

In the bygone Community Civil Readiness days, it may have been a reservoir or water-treatment plant, a cylindrical concrete pit, fifty feet in diameter and at least twenty deep, under bulky turbines and fans.

It was something else, now.

Something with weird waxlike formations built up in the center, clinging to the walls, depending from criss-crossing metal walkways... the substance congealed-looking, cloudy-creamy, marbled and translucent...strange liquids brimming in irregular pools and hollows...shadows moving within oblongs and bulges and bubbles...dotted with obscured and suspended shapes, occlusions like pieces of fruit in a gelatin dessert, like bugs trapped in amber...

While there he was, standing above it on a ledge, with his dick out, his dick in his hand, sticky-wet with fresh cum still dribbling from the slit, gloving his palm, oozing between his fingers.

As, below him, in the darkness, luminous things moved.

As they wallowed, and squirmed.

And hungered.

CHAPTER SEVENTEEN
REVULSION

Images flashed through Marty's mind, none of them quite right but each of them in some way close.

Lifting a rock to find writhing pale grubs underneath. Maggots in the slimy bottom of a garbage can. Slugs on a sidewalk after a storm. The one time in his life he'd gone fishing, being handed a plastic tub filled with slick knotted tangles of worms. Ants roiling crazily in a kicked anthill. Those videos you saw on nature documentaries, schools of fish grouped in a shimmering undersea ball, or a billowing jellyfish swarm.

As he, Dev, and Spence reeled Jake backward from the edge of the landing, it was all too obvious what the teeming mass at the bottom of the stairwell was doing.

Feeding.

Feeding on what Jake had just spurted over them.

"Makin' it *rain!*" Spencer cried in a lunatic cackle.

Converging, crowding, the way ducks and pigeons did when someone scattered a fistful of breadcrumbs, the way guppies or koi rose to a sprinkle of flakes into an aquarium.

Feeding.

Competing.

Survival of the fittest.

Fighting.

Marty knew—they all knew—what they were seeing.

It was *that* room, there was one just like it in every game, on every sewer or factory map; that big round room with its layers of walkways and weird lighting and dangerous drops. Usually where the mission objective would be found, or the final boss battle waited, or both.

Most of the things down there were no bigger than bullfrogs, the texture and pale-greenish color of that glow-

143

in-the-dark slime-putty you could get in a cheap plastic egg from the quarter machines at the grocery store.

Only, moving. Alive.

Like living boogers, mucusy phlegm, runny snot-rockets. The keening, unformed baby-bird clamor of their hunger and greed—

more more more more

—caused him to think absurdly of those seagulls in that fish movie from when he was a kid, mine-mine-mine, but same basic idea.

A few others—larger, the jiggly-wobbly half-set jello molds of their lime green and blue raspberry brighter— had begun making their way up the walls and formations in a leechlike, inchwormy, reverse-Slinky kind of hunching undulation. Their feelers wavered. They left snail-trails.

From them, the urgent pulse of need was clearer and stronger.

Give feed grow give come to us come for us feed and fill we are one.

Elongated protrusions stretched from their narrower ends, probing-questing-seeking. Marty thought again of nature documentaries, anteater noses and elephant trunks, curling, prehensile.

"Let's *go!*" Devon said. "Let's get out of here!"

Nobody argued. They just fled, Jake cramming himself back into his pants on the run. They went without really knowing or caring which way they were headed. As long as it was *away*. Away from the…

lair nest hive den

…horror as fast as they could.

Stumbling, bumping into walls, tripping over debris. Barely able to see in the wild waving blurs of their phones. Hindering and helping each other in equal measure.

Marty's foot slipped and he skidded to a knee, barking with pain. Jake caught his hand before he plowed chin-first into the floor. He was already up and running again by the time his brain registered what that tepid, tacky moistness squishing against his palm and fingers must be.

Trying not to puke, trying not to gag and caw with disgust, he scrubbed his hand on his leg. It was on his *skin*, who knew when he'd be able to *wash*...washing wouldn't be *enough*, he wanted to *boil* it from the forearm down, boil it and then douse it in Purell or something...it was on him, it was *on* him, what if he accidentally touched his face... *eeuuuurgh*...

They ran.

So turned around now, no idea where they were.

How damn big was this place? An emergency shelter or survival bunker, okay, but, seriously, dudes, this was *Fairmont*, not a major city, not a military base! And would it have killed them, when they built it, to stick some You-Are-Here signs on the walls along with the rah-rah patriotic stuff?

Finally, when they reached an intersection where there were no signs of pursuit and no movement but their own, Jake signaled a stop. For someone who'd almost jumped down a pit full of demon slug-leeches—demon slug-leeches onto which he'd shot a copious splattering wad—and had to be yanked back from the literal brink, he evidently still saw himself as team leader.

The true irony of it being, well, he was right. Who else could be? Not Devon the new kid, sure as hell not Spencer Bodean, and as for Marty? Yeah, that was a laugh.

"We need to rest a minute," Jake said. "Catch our breath. Dev, Marty, turn off your phones. Conserve the batteries. Is everybody okay? You guys saved my ass back there, thanks. What's our situation?"

Spence laughed hollowly. "Totally fucked."

"There were so many," Devon said. "Why were there so many? Didn't we just summon one?"

"Dude," said Marty, shaking his head. "We don't know what we did."

"We know it worked," said Jake. "A little too well, yeah, but it also means there's got to be a way to get rid of them."

Not that anyone currently had any brilliant ideas. And not like they could go to the internet for answers; they couldn't even use their phones as phones.

145

They debated briefly whether or not to try holing up in one of the storerooms or old offices, maybe barricading the door from the inside. But the prospect of being cornered, caught in a dead end with no other avenue of escape, was even more nerve-wracking than the feeling of being open and exposed. At least the intersection offered some choices.

It also offered one of the useless drinking fountains, as if to taunt and remind them how thirsty they were. Marty remembered—it seemed ages ago!—tucking a can of soda in his jacket pocket before leaving the apartment...but when he checked, he found it must've fallen out somewhere along the way in their mad crazy chase.

All he had left were two snack-cakes, mashed flat in their wrappers. He divvied the pieces and offered them around.

"Hostess fuckin' roadkill," Spence observed, not that he let it stop him from taking some.

"At least it's not the kind with coconut flakes," Devon said.

"Yeah, you're welcome," said Marty. "Glad I shared."

"Thanks, bro, seriously," Jake said.

Spencer and Devon mumbled their thanks too, through mouthfuls of crumbled cake and crème filling. Feeling a little less disgruntled, Marty scooped the last clumps from the packaging.

Only as he was scraping the thin pieces of cardboard with his thumb to get every bit did it occur to him the treat tasted funny, and only as he licked a smear of frosting from his hand did he realize why.

The reason he didn't puke or scream was because his system was trying to do both at the same time. A swelling logjam of pressure like the worst heartburn and stalled burp ever stuck in his chest.

"Marty?"

"You okay, man?"

"If you're gonna hurl, don't do it here!"

He lurched from the wall against which he'd been leaning and blundered blindly down one of the halls, turning random corners, groping for doorhandles, hoping for a bathroom.

The plumbing wouldn't work, he knew that, any sinks would be as useless as the drinking fountains they'd passed. But, a toilet bowl he could puke in, and maybe *some* water left in the tank, never mind if it was a rusty puddle seventy years old, as long as he could rinse and spit, wash his hands!

Or an office with a water-cooler, that wasn't so far-fetched! Any decently-designed game would have had something! Didn't have to be heal-packs or mana-boosts or ammo, but *some* sort of damn resource!

From behind him, he heard the others, Devon calling worriedly, Spence griping how this was the exact fuckin' thing they were *not* supposed to do and Beth really would give them no end of shit for actin' just like retards in horror movies after all, and Jake seconding Spence with a we-have-to-stick-together/don't-split-the-team pep talk.

The nerve of *that*, after his earlier wait-here-guys business!

The next door Marty came to was ajar, momentum carrying him through and into one of those long barracks-style dormitories. He could tell because a dim yellowish light came from yet another door at the far end, casting shadows of cots and bunk beds lined in rows down the sides.

His logjammed conflicting urges to scream and to puke got shunted aside by a colossal overpowering demand for escape. For freedom, for the outside world, the above-world, the real world where awful shit like this didn't happen and a dude could enjoy a snack-cake without getting a mouthful of another dude's cum!

"Marty!"

"Fuck! Which way did he go?"

"C'mon, we gotta find him!"

Pausing to wait for them to catch up now that the end was in sight seemed like a really stupid way to have salvation pricktease-snatched from him at the last second. Marty ran past the bunks and through the next door, finding himself in—

WTF really?

the fallout shelter equivalent of a goddamn gymnasium,

147

jogging track, basketball-tennis-vollyball courts, instant flashback to high school all over again—

—shorts and sweat and clumsiness Coach and his whistle Coach and his commands to hustle up strip down hit the showers locker room satiric hoots at boy-boobs and snap-flick damp towel stinging ass-welts and sneering snickers FUCK YOU TROY CAHILL—

He stumbled again and this time there was no Jake to offer him a 'helping' hand.

The sound of his flab thwack-walloping the gym floor was something else that hadn't changed at all in the intervening years; but, no, he got endless shit for preferring to stay home playing video games instead of going out for sports!

Like it was any wonder he'd rather do something he could be good at! Where he could be someone else! Where he didn't have to endure girls laughing at him pitying him calling him a creep!

Where he didn't have to face the constant rejection and humiliation, where he might stand a *chance*...

A chance why wait on chance why wait when what you want is so near? Be as you are as you wish as you desire.

Marty froze, even as a soothing warmth washed over him.

Are you here to come for me again?

The voice, god, that Mila Kunis voice.

I know how you want me. I sense your desire, Hellslayer. Your arousal. I can feel it. Taste it. You ache for my touch. For my kiss.

Llylth, lush-bodied, crimson-skinned...hair trailing and billowing and swirling like ebony smoke...the sway of her hips and the lithe curling of her tail...the hot caress of her breath in his ear...the teasing caress of her clever, supple, forked tongue...

How your blood surges, how your cock stiffens, how your hardness throbs! Begging to be taken. Pleasured. Isn't that what you want? What you crave?

But she wasn't real! It was a lie, an illusion, some sort of mind-trick or hallucinogenic head-trip!

Shall I go on my knees for you, Hellslayer? A queen, on her knees, supplicant to your lustful urges? My mouth yours to claim, to fill and to fuck, to spill your seed as I swallow it down, every drop?

A dream. A fantasy. A sad, sick, desperate, pathetic joke! Right, like he cared, so the hell what?

None of that matters now. None of that matters. Only this. Only now. We need you. I need you.

Looking down, looking down, and for a moment yes there yes Llylth the demon-queen on her knees, wings draped, dark claws lifting away the codpiece of his Eldritch-forged armor—an ultra-rare drop, triple-enhanced for speed and deflection, 4 levels of banefire absorbtion, 20% strength boost, and full damage set bonuses to all Tier-9 weaponry—to release his Tier-10 weapon, it was huge, proud and thick, a massive polearm of man-meat.

Use me, Hellslayer. Use me for your pleasure. Fuck and fill me, pour your rich salt life-milk, flood me with it.

Seeing the admiration, the eagerness in her eyes. The sensation as she slid him into her mouth, slid him deeper than deep all the way all the way and the hot slick wet suction...

Feel the lust feel the pleasure feel how I suck yes suck drink swallow, feed me, give me of the milk of your loins.

Looking down, and it was *him* on his knees, pants and underwear bunched mid-thigh, gut drooping from under his GTA t-shirt. Groping for purchase on a slippery mass as he drove his ordinary unimpressive never-touched-by-a-real-girl dick into...

*Fill me I hunger **we** hunger...*

Hearing the gooshy arrhythmic slap-smackings, his own fevered grunts and groans.

We hunger yes yes we hunger feed me feed us feed us all...

As, from all around him, sinuous sliding aquamarine luminescence, more of them closed steadily in.

149

CHAPTER EIGHTEEN
DIVERSION

Mart-O, surrounded.

Busy with one of the neon-jelly fleshlights, giving her mouth—or whatever—a clumsy, frantic, furious humping. Laughing as he did so, laughing or maybe sobbing, maybe screaming; Spence couldn't tell.

What he could tell was that the other ones, squelching and schlorping their eager way toward him, didn't look likely to wait patient and take turns. They were gonna swarm his ass, bury him, suffocate and drown him in a quivering mound of goo even as they cocksucked him to death.

"Jake! Dev! This way!" he shouted as he ran, shoes squeaking—who the fuck puts a basketball court underground?

And where was fuckin' Daryl with his crossbow when it'd do some damn good? Puncture those bladdersack bitches, pop 'em like water balloons…water balloons filled with jizz, nastiest fuckin' pinatas ever…

But they hadn't brought weapons or any of that. Never thinking they'd need it, morons that they were; Beth had been right, ever even *seen* a horror movie? Should have known, should have fuckin' *known*, and instead they were scrambling around down here trapped in the dark with fuckin' *dozens* of these things!

He could smell them, their scent thick and steamy in the air, that yeasty-sour-briny-sweet-spunky-musky-doughy scent, fuckin' vile yet also oddly a turn-on, and if he got too close they would get him the way they'd got Marty, they'd turn into the Harmon sisters again or his cousin Jolene or whatever other sick shit they dredged up from his filthy-fuckin'-mind…

His shoes squeaked again as he skidded to a halt. Jake and

150

Devon rushed up with their phone-beams sweeping back and forth, not adding much to what filtered down from a single wire-caged yellow bulb somehow still surviving overhead.

"Be ready to grab him!" Spence said. "I got a plan!"

Neither of their expressions conveyed much confidence in *that*, thank you very much, but Spence was already in action. Button, zipper, go; Jake wasn't the only one who could whip it on out.

"Hey!" he yelled. "Yo! Cumslut! Jizzabel! Whatever the fuck your names are! You want somma-*this*?" He waggled his junk at them, dandling the ol' scrote like a bag of choice plums at the produce stand, pumping a curled fist up and down his semi-chub to help it along.

"Spencer-what-the-hell!" Devon cried.

It was a plan, though, and it worked—several of the glowing green slug-blobs immediately diverted their course toward Marty and homed in on him.

"Yeah, that's right!" He kept yelling as he zigzagged and sidestepped, gaining more and more succubus attention. "I got gallons to spare, ladies, right here on tap!"

They surged at him in a rolling, roiling wave. Spence backpedaled—shit, they were fast!—and had a moment where he almost fell—that would have been it, fucked for sure—but then regained his footing and managed to set a pretty decent backwards pace, still waving his dick at them.

"Check it," he whooped to the others. "Pied Piper of Cumsluts!"

Crazy as fuck, but it was working. They were following him. Not all, but enough to let a bedraggled and shocked-looking Marty extricate himself—yeah, they were probably all bound for the loony bin after this, this was beyond, just fuckin' *beyond.*

He squeezed out a few pre-drops, which sent them into a total frenzy, totally steamrollering and bulldozing each other to be first to the goods. Making moist, smoochy-slurpy noises, they lapped and vacuumed up their prize.

"Here goes!" Spencer shouted. "Cummin' to the rescue!"

No need to be discreet; he let fly in a wide, spattering

arc. They went wilder than teen girls at a boy-band concert, but he right away saw that it wouldn't be enough. He hadn't gone limp—if anything was harder than ever—but he didn't know how long he could keep it, so to fuckin' speak, up.

Dev ran to help Marty. Jake ran to join Spencer.

"That was terrible, bro."

"Got a better idea?"

"No."

They got a system going, world's most fucked-up relay race, track and field in the Jackoff Olympics, going for the gold, U-S-A! U-S-A! With him and Jake trotting backwards, trying to spurt and splash and scatter a trail of distraction, while Dev and Marty forged ahead with their phones.

Spence threw Jake a sidelong look. "Can you fuckin' believe this shit?"

"No," Jake said, missing neither stride nor stroke.

"Maybe we're dreaming," said Devon.

"Or trippin' balls," Spence suggested.

"We're crazy," Marty said.

Somehow, crazy or dreaming or trippin' balls, they finally gained enough ground—or spread enough distraction—to leave their pursuers far enough behind that he and Jake could put their dicks away and face forward.

Not that they knew where the hell they were. It was a clusterfuck of the first order. Those things were *breeding* down here, they had built a fuckin' *lair* down here, that one room had been some kind of anthill-in-progress, a slug-blob beaver den or wasp's nest or something.

"What do we do?" Devon asked, after a minute or so.

They'd slowed to a walk and gone back to minimal phone-light to save batteries—still no fuckin' bars or signal, of course.

"Keep your shit together," Jake said.

"But there's so many of them! What if they get out?"

"News flash, dude, they can already get out," Marty said. "How else do you think they've been visiting us?"

"Maybe not just us," Spencer said. "They're that fuckin' hungry, for all we know they're *visitin'* all over town."

Horrified contemplation, while Dev and Jake in particular looked like they wanted to object, but that'd be some pie-in-the-sky level you-wish right there. Go big or go home; when a bunch of retards started fuckin' around with demon-magic, what the fuck would you expect?

"Somebody would have said something..." Devon began, then trailed off.

Because yeah right, who? Said what? How long had it taken even the four of them to realize what was goin' on, and they'd caused it. Anyone else might just be thinkin' they got super-lucky, braggin' about it at most, or havin' themselves some crazy-ass wet dreams.

"Dude," said Marty. "Dude, that's...that's so wrong."

"Okay, guys, look," said Jake. "We can deal with that later, okay? First, we have to get out of here."

"And hey." Spence shrugged. "Free epic blow-your-mind blowjobs; succubus suckfest, half of fuckin' Fairmont should be thankin' us!"

Jake nodded, as if trying to convince himself there was indeed a bright side. "Yeah...yeah, it could be worse...not as if they're actually *hurting* anybody, right?"

"I guess." The new kid didn't sound very convinced.

Which of course was their goddamn *cue* to turn a corner and see a pair of splayed *feet* sticking out from an open door. Feet in grimy, grubby old shoes...attached to legs in grimy, grubby old pants...leading up to a...

Then, after at least two maybe three of them screamed like pussies—Spence hoped, but without much optimism, that *he* hadn't been one—they were running again.

As they did, he caught a glimpse and yes-in-fuckin'-deed that was a body. A body, a corpse, a stiff in the other sense, the bucket been kicked, the farm been bought. All shriveled up and dry, sticklike scarecrow bundle of beef jerky, but for all that he was willing to bet it hadn't been here mummified for five hundred years like King-fuckin-Tut; the stink was too ripe, fresh, and real for that.

Besides, it sure as shit looked like that one tall skinny bald fuck, the boss-man leader of the Shelter Park bum brigade, the one who'd tried to help Beth play peacekeeper when Spencer had been ready to rumble with that numbfuck bigmouth called Tater.

The next one sure as shit, even in the jittery flashes of phones, looked like the weirdo with the parka and the tinfoil hat. Stuck sprawl-propped against a wall all rotted teeth gaped mouth, not the well-chick from *The Ring* but the other one, the closet-chick, except instead of being slimy, he was dried out, eyeballs shriveled-up raisins in the bottoms of empty sockets.

Mummified and King-fuckin'-Tut, he'd been closer on that…the other mummy movie with the prim-sexy librarian babe and the cowboys who got all their fluids drained dry and hadn't he just thought that, earlier, only half-joking, about Mart-O getting sucked to death?

Which was what must've happened to the bums, what with the way their Goodwill-reject pants were undone—there was the asshole who'd hit them up for dollars or smokes, and Jesus-*fuck* had they *eaten* his whole fuckin' crotch? Spence had seen more meat left on a chicken carcass after one of Nana Nell's Sunday suppers! But, bad as that was, somehow the bum's dying O-face rictus was what was gonna haunt Spence's dreams.

He heard the others reacting with more cries of shock and revulsion, and his own words—*that's what we been stickin' our dicks in*—came back to haunt him with a fuckin' vengeance. How long until *they* ended up like that? Goddamn feeding frenzies and yeah maybe what a way to go but no thanks!

And then there was Tater.

Fuckin' *Tater*, who'd cracked wiseass about Spence's momma, but Tater would be crackin' wiseass about nobody's momma now, or anything else, ever again. Him and his just-say-no-drugs're-bad-m'kay, for all the good *that'd* done him, the drunk ol' fuck, draped faceup across an overturned filing cabinet with dead claw-hands and straggle-haired straggle-bearded head dangling.

If there was more to see, Spence didn't wanna look. Because, if there was more to see, it might be fuckin' *Brendan*, and douche-fuckstick or not, even he didn't deserve endin' up like that.

As for the rest of Fairmont, he had a feeling that blow-your-mind blowjobs thing wasn't going to earn them any thanks after all. Once people found out who was responsible for...what, the succubus apocalypse? Good luck making a TV series, unless on HBO or some shit where they could show full-frontal every damn episode...

He realized his thoughts weren't making a whole lot of sense, the adrenaline whipping through his system really stir-frying his brains. He also realized they were slowing, staggering to a halt, needing to stop before they just fuckin' keeled over.

Devon was shaking. Jake kept twitching around to check every direction for the glimmering blue-green telltale signs of pursuit.

Marty, bent over with his hands on his knees, heaving for breath, managed to glance over at Spencer. Spence, who'd sagged into a corner wondering if it was too late to start actually going to church or something, sort of half-grinned, expecting Mart-O to thank him for the save back there.

Instead, with a really sarcastic sneer, Mart-O was all, "Let's summon a succubus, he said. It'll be fun, he said."

"Shut the fuck up!" retorted Spencer, indignant.

"*You're* the fuck-up!"

Shit might've gone down then for real, but Jake intervened. "*Both* of you, shut up already!"

INTERLUDE: VIGNETTES #6

Hey, that's where we came in...back in the prologue at the beginning of the book!

We left it there, with the guys trying to escape from the underground lair, having discovered the problem is a whole lot worse than they'd realized.

But now, the rest of the story's caught up to that point. You-the-reader probably have a pretty good idea of what's going on. You may be speculating, even anxious, to see what happens next.

Which means this is the perfect place for another of these obnoxious goddamn Interludes!

***

But, first:

"Looks like some kind of secreted resin."

"Yeah, but secreted from *what*?"

Hey, we were all thinking it.

And I'll have you know, it was a dire struggle indeed not to have someone holler, "Get away from him, you bitch!" in the previous chapter. Or "they mostly come at night, mostly"...a "game over, man, game over!" *may* have sneaked into the book somewhere already; I'm not sure.

I mean, shit, it's only about the most quotable movie in history. I'll hardly deny there are certain derivative elements. Besides, what would you expect from a shameless fanfiction hack?

Onward!

***

Ah, the succubus.

People get all hung up on the sexy demon chick image, the psychic shape-shifter with nymphomania and telepathy, the veritable girl of your wet-dreams. Naked babes with cute little batwings, cute little horns, sinuous little tails. Slutty She-Devil Halloween costumes. They're in the *Monster Manual*. Half a generation of nerdy guys first became aware of nipples that way.

Sexy, sexy demon chicks.

As our boys have learned, to their sorrow and peril, such isn't exactly the case. The images are only that: images. Mirages, sensory hallucinations, mental illusions.

Jake was right about there being a pheromone component, but it can work as a contact agent as well. Particularly when the more sensitive body parts or delicate mucous membranes are involved.

We've all heard of those colorful little frogs whose skin seeps psychedelic toxins. Pufferfish and other weird sea creatures release nerve toxins; our clever friends the dolphins have even figured out how to use measured doses of the stuff to get high.

Remember we were talking about mermaids earlier? Hey, maybe there's something to those ancient mariner tales beyond sunstroke, sea-blindness, scurvy and rum. Mermaids…sirens…definitely a siren-like quality to our demons here, too.

Mainly, though, they're like bees.

Succubus-bees.

Succubees? No, that's stupid. Sounds like a bad restaurant venture, Hooters trying to go somewhat upscale.

The correct plural would be succubi. From the Latin, by the way; look at us learning more about languages and linguistics and philology and stuff. This book's just all kinds of educational, isn't it?

***

As for Llylth, the lush and lovely seductive *Hellslayer* demon-queen, well, what do you want? She's a video game character. Over-the-top voluptuous boob physics and absurdly revealing outfits go with the territory. Especially for the wicked temptresses.

Vampirella, for example...her costume, what there is of it, was designed to be so skimpy and utterly naughty there was no possible way anybody could argue she wasn't full-bore evil. That was back in the late 1960s.

Soon, though, it wasn't just the villainesses, femme fatales, and dirty bad girls. Soon, even the heroines were dressing to thrill. You know what they had to do? They had to go back and try to find ways to make Vampirella's outfit even sluttier.

We've had chainmail bikinis and boob windows and Mystique in body paint. Yeah, I would have preferred her in the white gown with the skull belt, but I also would have preferred flirty swashbuckler Nightcrawler, and anyway that's not the point...the point is, the people who argue how it makes sense for the character to be naked never seem to have realism problems with the way Wolverine's jeans miraculously survived at the end of the third X-Men movie.

Tangent. Sorry. Anyway, it's all about ethics in game journalism, amirite?

No, wait. It's about Llylth, the succubus-queen.

And what else has queens? Besides certain alien xenomorphs, of course?

***

Their lair, it really is like a giant subterranean infernal beehive.

Only, it isn't wax. What they process and store isn't honey. The 'nectar' they collect does not come from flowers.

Let's call it semencomb. Cumcomb may be funnier, but is just awkward to say.

The structure of their society is hivelike too, with the

busy little succubus-drones going out to gather the goods and bring it home. Some for sustenance, of course; it's nutrient-rich, packed with proteins, vitamins, and minerals.

Not that it'll likely be the next big superfood diet craze, sorry fellas…whatever overall health benefits there may be, a typical serving size of about a teaspoon per isn't going to put any supplement companies out of business anytime soon.

For a succubus colony, however, it's another story.

***

Speaking of another story, there is one aspect of succubus lore that tends to be ignored or overlooked.

That'd be the incubus.

Not nearly so well-known.

So not nearly so well-known, in fact, that, once—and this is no-shit legit, check Snopes—a top-brand company thought it'd make a nifty brand name for a line of ladies' running shoe. Seriously. The Reebok Incubus. Look it up.

Someone must've done just enough thesaurus research to figure it was a cool-sounding synonym for 'spirit' and not quite enough to realize the more common definition is more like 'male sex vampire.'

Oops. Slight marketing blooper, but they caught it in time to pull their overly-expensive sneakers off the market.

Male sex vampire. Funny that, because a succubus is more usually considered a sex *demon*, with the vampire angle downplayed or left off.

And male sex vampire, hey, that's become pretty much synonymous with sexy male vampire. Down the torrid rabbit hole of paranormal romance you go, first they're all brooding and dark and angsty and then they become sparkly little bitches and what the hell *happened*, people?

Ahem. Anyway.

Male or female doesn't matter, because they're neither. Or both. Depending. Depending on circumstance, occasion, and need. It's the exact same being, performing various different functions.

***

Again, like bees.
    Collection.
    Production.
    Construction.
    Protection.
    Implantation.
    Incubation.
    That last one...Word Origins for $800, Alex...funny
how it just all fits together, isn't it?

***

And remember Enoch, our eunuch? We were talking about
him earlier.
    Speaking of linguistics and word origins, by the way, the
term 'eunuch' is from the Greek.
    Okay, sure, we could go with *castrato*, which is Italian,
but that term usually applies more to singing and the musical
aspect, and implies angelic blond choir boys with the sweet
voices of ultimate purity.
    Enoch Shaw, not so much.
    Also, naming someone Enoch? Then making him a
eunuch? That's just insult to injury. Would anybody really
have blamed him if he *had* killed his parents?
    Anyway, Enoch the eunuch.
    Who's obsessed with making babies...with playing God.
    Or, in some cases, with doing God one better.
    He loves making women pregnant. He's really good at
it, too. Especially women who otherwise might never have
babies, for whatever reason. He loves it. Gives him a real
sense of power and potency. Sure, maybe he has no penis,
maybe he has no scrotum or testicles or sperm of his own...
but why let that stop him?
    In a sense, that almost makes *him* an incubus.
    A eunuch incubus, how about that?

CHAPTER NINETEEN
SUSPENSION

He'd tried fighting. He'd tried begging.

Neither worked.

They were too strong, too many to fight. His pleas went ignored or unheard.

They only obeyed *Her*.

She Who Must Be Obeyed? What was that even from? Some book, or some British thing, as best he can remember.

All he knew was, his mother had a sleepshirt with that printed on it in glittery gold cursive, with the image of a crown. Also a coffee mug and a framed print for her office at the clinic. 'Gag' gifts from the staff. Ha-ha, yes, so funny.

He'd even tried bargaining. Ready to sell out his parents, ruin the family business, screw over the entire town and indeed the whole damn world.

That didn't work, either. They didn't want it processed, in vials, frozen and cold. Maybe in a pinch, maybe to store up like squirrels with nuts for the winter, but They far preferred having it fresh from the source.

She was like some giant, gelatinous Terminator. Couldn't be argued with, couldn't be reasoned with, didn't feel pity or remorse or fear or whatever. Just hunger. Her hunger, Her need and Her lust.

And wouldn't stop until he was dead?

He wished it was that simple.

He wished he was dead.

She wouldn't let him die. *They* wouldn't let him. Somehow, They kept keeping him alive.

Feeding him…

An all-liquid diet.

Thick, warm, and creamy. Like blended milk and honey, manna from Heaven, but it wasn't honey and it sure as hell wasn't milk.

Force-feeding him, because, like a stubborn baby in a highchair, he'd refused to willingly partake of the puddingy offerings, and spat back out whatever got into his mouth.

So, now, when They fed him, They did so via makeshift gastric tube. Each would ooze up to him, extrude a long thin tendril to worm up his nose and down his throat—slick and terrible invasive sinal violation!—and pump the goo-jelly in steady, pulsating streams directly into his stomach.

At least he couldn't taste it. At least there was that.

Unless he managed to vomit.

He wasn't sure which was worst. The feeling of a sloshing, full, contented belly…the murky flavor mixed with acids gurgling back up…or the knowledge of what it was.

No, the knowledge of what it was, that was the worst.

Brendan hung helpless in Her soft, pendulous mass and wanted to die.

Around him, around Her, the others went about their various duties.

Some were builders, depositing gluey globs of the most waxlike substance, shaping it, smoothing it in layers. Reminding him of those immense termite mounds found in Africa, ten or twelve feet tall, constructed of chewed mud and secretions— *spermite mounds*, he thought, but it wasn't funny.

Some tended the hollows where the not-honey brimmed in pools, ripening and steeping and fermenting…sorted by variety, color, vintage…filled vats being sealed over to properly age…like a weird version of a winery or distillery… put *that* on your tours, Fairmont wine-snobs!

Some were nurses, taking care of the squirmy larval tadpole-things which hatched in runny caviar torrents from the brussels-sprout pustules lining Her sides. Some served as personal attendants, some as guards and scouts.

And some were collectors. Seeking, gathering, bringing.

What They brought, She sampled.

The salt-life-seed, the nectar, the man-milk.
The mind-milk.

Echoes and images. Dreams. Fantasies. Memories. Cut scenes of the subconscious, the guilty conscience, the dark nasty underside of the psyche.

He knew them, most of them, and half-recognized the rest.

There were his friends…the friends who'd run away and abandoned him, not such good friends, fuck you guys anyway, fuck you! Enjoy your imaginary Cynthia-Lynne and demon queen and trailer trash freakshow and…Beth? Had that been Beth? But Devon, new kid good boy virgin too chicken too scared?

Jake's neighbor with the shaved head and neck tats… had a thing for lips, a lip-fetish, Avon catalogs with close-up after close-up of luscious full lips lipstick colors coral blush rich burgundy frosted peach red velvet succulent pink, lips lips lips wet and pouting parting shiny plump, actresses and models, Kardashian, Beyonce, Jolie, internet duck-face selfies, nothing else just the lips just a big ball of lips opening opening painted lips printing their lipmarks at the base of his cock—also tattooed, holy shit, the dude had neck tats *and* groin tats, how must that have *hurt!*—but the lips sliding gliding riding up and down plum and crimson and sweet clear gloss as the ball revolved and revolved.

There was Coach…Coach and Roxie? Sucked off by his dog? Man's best friend, okay, great, noble and all, but really that should only go so far!

And Beth's boss, big bad black Rodney, liking vulnerable white women with wounded-shy eyes, getting them down on their knees between his muscular thighs, take it you take it all you throat it throat it good, and finishing off with fist-pumping facials pearl necklaces dousing their pillowy tits, yeah you love that dontcha yeah baby…

There was Sebastian Abbott, rich-playboy hot-shit hotel mogul sleazeball, as if he didn't already have all the pussy he could handle, mistresses and affairs and one-night-stands. But evidently none of them were giving him what he really wanted, and he normally had to save that release for trips to the city where he could buy discretion because there weren't going to be many ladies in Fairmont who'd agree to provide watersports and scatplay and throwjobs—

Brendan almost did vomit then, stopped only by the gross certainty Abbott might get off on it if he knew.

More ordinary fantasies predominated, hitchhikers cheerleaders strippers schoolgirls pajama parties anonymous hookups drunk mistakes glory holes naughty nurses...more people from town, former classmates, shopkeepers—was that Devon's dad?—and one of the nerdy poindexter assistants from his parents' clinic enjoying some cartoon action with Betty and Veronica.

Then the dark sick stuff again, the pain yes the pain, some old man, wizened and paralyzed, bedridden...and the bitch with her cigarettes and cruel smile twisting the ash-smolder-embers into his wrinkled leathery skin...it hurts oh it hurts but it's all he can feel...he can *feel* he can feel *something,* something stiffening for the first time in years... and she recoils in loathing hatred disgust...you filthy old fuck!...to punish him she grinds it out there, but joke's on her and the squirt hits the bitch right in the eye!

Troy? Was that Troy Cahill laying down a little vindictive date-rape on a passed-out Cynthia-Lynne?

And here, some other guy standing beside a bed...the bathroom light is on and he can see her burrowed sleeping under the covers...he's known, he's always known, deep in his heart he's always known...the lying, faithless whore... her and her *migraines,* and he'd been such a sap...slaving away while she fools around behind his back, probably laughing at him, laughing with her lovers...but no more of that, no, no more...one last headache, he'd give her a migraine to remember...bash her brains open and skull-fuck her as she dies!

All this and more, T*hey* brought back to the nest, back to the lair, to the hive, to *Her.*

Feeding and growing.

Becoming stronger.

Gathering. Storing.

Treating and transforming. Making ready. Making ripe.

Preparing for the next phase, the next step, the next stage of their cycle.

Meanwhile, Brendan's friends—his so-called, asshole, *friends!*—had returned.

To look for him, they told themselves. To fix their mistakes and make right their wrongs.

How's that working out for you, fellas? he thought. *Not too well, huh?*

Maybe, if they were lucky, they'd end up like the homeless creeps who'd wandered down here.

More likely, they'd end up like Brendan himself.

After all, Devon and Spencer and Marty and Jake had been right there involved in the summoning, too. Had each contributed, participated, taken part in the ritual.

The five of them, together, had Called.

And She had Answered.

He hung there, suspended immobile in the bathwater-warm albumen, aware of the softening bagginess and sloughing of his skin, of the way his body hair had long since dissolved—fingernails and toenails, too. Aware of the way his bones felt spongy and weightless and weak, so that even if he was suddenly somehow freed, his limbs would flail and flop limp as noodles.

And aware, vividly, horribly aware, of what had already happened to his balls.

Words like blanched, peeled, poached, and separated sprang to mind. Along with medical words like tubules and vesicles, which did not go well with words like unraveled, uncoiled, unspooled, and drifting.

Even if he *was* suddenly somehow freed...

Yeah, all he would want, all he would beg and pray for, was death.

CHAPTER TWENTY
EVACUATION

Lines of murky red, dim, seemingly floating in the gloom.

Lines forming symbols.

Familiar symbols.

Letters.

Spelling out that most magic of magic words.

EXIT.

What Spence, in the lead, had seen first and pointed out to the rest of them.

"Hey! Fuck yeah!" he'd cried.

"Ohthankgod."—Marty.

"Told you it was this way! Let's get out of here!"—Jake.

"Fuckin' A."—Spencer.

Get out, yes. But then what? Who'll believe us?—Devon, not aloud.

Those questions could wait. Discussion later. Anywhere but here.

They hadn't gone half the distance toward the beckoning beacon, the promise of salvation, when the sounds reached them again. Murmuring, chuckling, rustling, a low and intimate whispering.

Feminine sounds, sounds to sway and stroke and seduce. Cooing and crooning.

Sleek. Terrible. Supple. Sexy.

None of them spoke. Spencer didn't bother to swear. They just ran again, ran like hell, ran like rabbits, ran in a headlong panicked final sprint.

As, behind them, clear blue-green gleams appeared, rippling shimmers of sun-on-tropical-shallows turquoise, an enticing and intoxicating promise, wonderful wet warmth, and a shining, deadly, hellish hunger.

Ahead was the EXIT sign, mounted above a door. A

thick emergencies-only-alarm-*will*-sound kind of door, with a heavy pushbar and an inset rectangular window of double-paned, wire-reinforced glass.

Jake and Spencer, neck-and-neck at the finish line, hit the pushbar simultaneously with the heels of their hands without slowing their pace.

It would have looked great, flawless choreography, if it had worked.

If the pushbar had budged. If the door had opened.

Instead, they both slammed straight full-tilt into it. The synchronized clanging thump of their bodies hitting metal didn't drown out the brittle snap-crackle-pop of at least a couple of wrists and one cell phone.

Spencer screeched. Jake howled. Devon managed to stop himself, only to have Marty plow into him from behind and turn the whole deal into a four-car pileup. By the time they sorted it out, the crooning murmurs and low chuckles seemed to be everywhere.

"It's locked!" Marty announced, trying the door.

"Thanks a shitload, Captain Obvious. My arm, fuckin' ow!"

With Jake's phone now broken and Marty's battery dead, they only had Devon's for light…that and the dull glow shed by the EXIT sign, which painted them with muddy reddish shadows. Devon shined his phone around.

Through the window was a tantalizing, teasing glimpse of freedom in the form of a dingy cinderblock stairwell. Leading who knew where, but leading *up*, and up was what mattered. Up, out, away.

He turned to shine it the other direction, suddenly remembering that damn *Five Nights at Freddy's* game Marty had made them watch Let's Plays of, and really wishing he hadn't.

The corridor stretched long and empty. He didn't see any—

Wait!

Or no, eyes playing tricks. Hyped imagination and nerves.

Maybe.

Something seemed to have moved. A sinuous, silken undulation. Coming closer.

He swept the phone around again, this time catching an eerie bluish-green gleam, a cat's-eye shimmer, a ripple like sunlight on tropical shallows.

No doubt this time, and Devon's heart gave a jump up his throat like a pinched watermelon seed. They were here. They were close. This time, he wouldn't be able to escape untouched. They weren't going to take no for an answer, not that he knew how much longer he'd be able to resist. How he'd done so this far was a mystery and a miracle he hadn't paused to examine.

"Break the window!" Jake said, grimacing through gritted teeth as he cradled both wrists to his chest.

"With what?" Marty banged a fist against the wire-reinforced glass. "I'd need like a sledgehammer!"

"Use that!" He jerked his head, sweat-damp hair falling in his eyes.

Devon looked where Jake indicated. Mounted on the wall was a fire extinguisher, the red paint of its tank chipped and peeling. Its bracket, caked with years of rust and corrosion, did not want to surrender its grasp.

Metal squealed as they struggled with it. Gritty flakes sifted to the floor. Devon scraped a knuckle, and Marty gashed his palm.

"Ah crap, we're going to need tetanus shots," Marty complained.

"Lockjaw, kind of the least of our problems," Jake said. "Fuckin' hurry, would you?"

"We're…unh!…trying!" Devon said.

The fire extinguisher tore loose with another tortured ear-splitting squeal, its abrupt release and plummeting weight making them both stagger. They almost dropped it—how about some broken toes to go with Spence and Jake's broken wrists?—but hefted it and drove its blunt butt-end into the window.

Thunk.

168

"Like you *mean* it!" Spence shouted.

"C'mon, guys!" Jake added.

Thunk! Clunk!

A brief and regretted glance over his shoulder showed Devon the scene he'd expected and dreaded—the hallway a wavery aquamarine radiance now, with succubus-blobs clinging to the floor-walls-ceiling, approaching in eager gooshing lollops, their warm bakery scent steaming in the air, yeast and eggs with saltier/meatier undertones, everything they'd put into that basin and more.

THUNK-crack!

"Fuck yeah! Like that!"

One ridiculous goddamn little fault-line, but he and Marty struck again with renewed effort—thunk-whack-crunch! Their battering ram was taking its own battering, metal denting, rust flakes and paint flakes showering in a grit; a race to see which would give way first. But the fault lines were spreading with brittle scratchy crackles, the window going cataract-opaque in patches, little crumbly glass-clods falling out.

Don't do this don't do this don't go don't run, stay stay stay, be with me be with us be with Her one with Her one with us.

"Get out of my head!" Devon heard himself shout.

"Shit, guys, faster!"

"Hurry!"

"We're screwed we're so screwed," sobbed Marty.

Then crack-CRUNCH and a cascade of chunks; some stayed caught in the wire webbing and some to the frame but a cool gust of dank concrete-scented air blew through with faint whistling noises—

—before the tank itself split, the fire extinguisher leap-spinning from their grasp, clanging to the floor, sputtering-spitting-spraying whatever the hell chemical foam they'd used in the 50's or whenever, choking clouds of weird whitish smoke through which the blue-green light turned into a disco-rave laser show.

Coughing, they attacked the reinforcing wire with their

bare hands, Dev and Marty, even Spencer tearing at it like a rabid mongoose.

While Jake—"Go on, guys, go!"—did the heroic noble-leader self-sacrifice charge, running back toward the thickest concentrations of turquoise glows.

"Jake!" Devon yelled.

But he kept going, his shadow looming and leaping distorted against the luminescent mist. It swallowed him up. He was gone.

"Jesus-fuck!" Spencer went from rabid mongoose to rabid wolverine.

Wires snapped and poinged from their moorings. Their fingers were thin-cut and sliced, ragged, stinging, slick with blood.

A terrible brightness loomed and grew in the corridor, casting its own shadows, an underwater sun, dawn as seen through a cresting tidal wave.

Marty abandoned his assault on the window, began wailing something—"Boss battle! Boss battle!" was what it sounded like—and flung himself into a fetal position with his arms wrapping his head.

They had forced open a gap in the reinforcing wire lattice, not much of a gap but enough for skinny Spence to decide it must be worth a shot; he boost-heaved himself into the opening, the poking wire ends ripping clothes and skin, drawing more blood. He thrashed like a fish in a net, kicked like a rabbit in a snare, and fell through headfirst in a scrabbling thud.

"Spencer!"

"I'm okay," he groaned, muffled. "Only my fuckin' face."

The boss-battle tsunami brightened and swelled, and it was visions of beauty bearing tempting treats, pies and cobblers, buttery-golden-fruity-melty-delicious, and girls, impossible dream girls, women, lingerie, the Victoria's Secret fashion show just for him…

Just for you all for you come to us come with us come for us yes come.

…and the little girl he'd had a crush on in grade school

and the teacher he'd had a crush on in grade school and characters from those fanart websites he needed to delete from his browser history...

Spence popped back up, split lips and busted nose, and thrust his good arm back through the hole. "Move your ass, new kid!"

Dev looked at Marty, but Marty was a lost cause even if he'd've been able to fit; Marty had given up.

Come to us be with us be with Me be with Her we are Her the pleasure the pleasure all you could desire all you could ever want endless pleasure let us love you and serve you and taste yes taste so rich and sweet.

He lunged for the window, seizing Spencer's hand, and it was his turn to kick-thrash-scrabble as the wires snagged at him like cat-claws, like thorns, like fishhooks. His shoulders wedged. He twisted and fought. His clothes tore. Spencer held tight, yanked with all his scant weight, and Devon screamed at a popping-gristle flare of pain in his elbow. The wires, now teeth of bear-traps, raked at his sides and chest.

Then something touched his feet.

Touched, flowed over, enfolded.

This was how bugs felt caught in syrupy tree-sap that would become amber...this was how it'd be to get caught in warm quicksand, or one of those thermal mineral mudbaths, or swallowing lava that somehow didn't burn.

Inexorable.

Spencer swore up a storm but the pull was too strong, their hands wrenched apart. Devon saw him fly backward, heard another painful thud, and stopped caring what happened to Spencer then because he was going backward himself, the wire teeth once again shredding clothes and flesh.

Into the engulfing, gelatinous, blue-green mass of Her embrace.

CHAPTER TWENTY-ONE
RESOLUTION

He dragged himself up the stairs, crawling, hitching along with one arm, leaving bloody handprints and smears. Each breath was like sandpaper. He couldn't see for shit in the dark but was glad, because dark meant *they* weren't hot on his heels and his ass.

Up the stairs, dragging, crawling, for what seemed like a vertical-fuckin'-mile.

Snuffling gasps of air through his mouth because his nose was a crushed, dripping mess. He'd lost a couple teeth somewhere in there too, he thought.

Up and up.

No idea what he'd find at the top but so what, who gave a fuck, he didn't care if he emerged in the basement of the Fairmont Town Hall or police station or courthouse…didn't care if it led to a round hatch in some island jungle *Lost* bullshit…as long as it was *out*, as long as it was *away*.

And yeah he'd abandoned his buddies, that was too bad, that was a genuine bitch-kitty shame; he could feel guilty later.

Spencer reached a landing, saw another shining red EXIT sign, and hauled himself tottering to his feet. He staggered toward the door.

If this one was locked, he was fucked.

Understood and agreed. He'd cannonball back down the stairwell to break his neck, if that was his only other option.

It had no window, not that he would have had any way to break one.

Tucking his broken wrist against his chest, he leaned on the pushbar.

Nothing.

Fuckin' nothing.

He pressed his forehead to the cool metal, eyes squeezed shut.

Okay.

Okay, fine then, fuck it.

Then, from the other side, he heard a grating, scraping rattle, and a heavy tumbler-click. The door juddered open, pulled as he still leaned against it. Spencer stumbled through, reeling, suddenly blinded by a splash of light like a bucketful of splash to the eyeballs.

Faceplant, which fuckin' hurt, not that he could do much more damage to his face at this point.

"*Spence*? Holy shit, Spencer, what happened? Where's the others?"

Beth?

Beth?

The *fuck*?

But, there she was, as he blinked his poor abused eyeballs into a more accustomed state for seeing. Beth, sliding her lockpicks back into her cell phone case, staring at him with an astounded expression.

"Beth...?"

"Jesus, Spencer, you look like homemade hell on a stick."

"... doing here?"

"Looking for you retards, what else? Yeah, I was pissed, but did you think I'd stay pissed forever? You're still my friends."

He laughed, but it hurt.

She peered past him, down the stairs. "Did they not make it? Are you telling me *you're* the Final Girl?"

Spence squinted up at her. "The fuck are you talking about?"

"In horror movies, dumbass. The Final Girl trope. The one who survives, the one who gets away." She smirked at him. "You know, the good girl, the virgin."

"Now wait just a damn minute," he said, mustering the scraps of his dignity. "Anybody's the Final-fuckin'-Girl around here, should've been Devon."

"I know," Beth said. "I thought it would be. But you left

173

him behind, ran out on him to save your own scrawny ass."

"Whuh…how did…?"

Her smirk widened to a triumphant smile, as a shimmering blue-green aura spread out around her. "But, you know what, Spencer Bodean? You're still utterly fucked."

INTERLUDE #7

Of course, you just knew something like that was going to happen. It's just the way these things work! The last-minute gotcha right at the end. When salvation and safety almost seem too good to be true.

Where's the real Beth, you might wonder? Oh, she's at home. Still plenty pissed at her friends, no matter what that mirage had to say.

She'll *stay* pissed at them a while longer, until it's obvious they're missing.

Until it's obvious other weird things are going on.

Like Troy Cahill jumping out his bedroom window, and the strange pictures found on his phone.

Like most of the men in town starting to act really distracted and strange.

Almost as if they're addicted, hypnotized, obsessed.

And then it'll start getting even weirder.

Remember, this was only the first phase. The summoning, the Call.

Once the succubus colony is established, thriving, and strong...once they've gathered and brought...stockpiled, and prepared...

Why, then it's time for the next stage.

The incubus stage.

When the unsuspecting ladies of Fairmont get their turn.

We've met or heard of a few of them already. Beth's mom, and Devon's...little miss saving-it-for-marriage Cynthia-Lynne...the hot lesbian high-school French teacher... Hank Vilstreet's wife...the evil Vivian Farcastle with her cigarettes...Beth herself...hell, Roxie the dog, why not...

Nothing like a whole host of surprise, unexpected, and even supposedly impossible pregnancies to shake things up.

175

Oh, and just to kick it up a notch, to raise the stakes and make everything worse? Let's look in across town at the clinic, *In Vitro Veritas*.

Where Brendan's dad has just discovered one of his employees made an unfortunate blooper.

A bunch of faulty fertility drugs weren't disposed of properly.

They were, in fact, illegally dumped.

Contaminating Fairmont's water supply.

"Oops," says the employee, a nerdy poindexter who hasn't been sleeping at all well thanks to a series of very vivid dreams involving Betty and Veronica, Daphne and Velma, Poison Ivy and Harley Quinn, etc.

"Oops?" echoes Dr. Enoch Shaw. "We've just turned every woman in town into a game of uterine pachinko, and you tell me 'oops'?"

You better believe he acts angry, and you better believe the poindexter is fired and will be scapegoated like whoa.

But the truth is, inwardly, privately, our eunuch couldn't be more thrilled!

What this all really boils down to is a blatant set-up for a sequel.

I'm thinking *Babydaddies of the Damned...*

(the 'oops,' setup for a sequel)

ABOUT THE AUTHOR

Christine Morgan is a crazy-cat-lady old frump who looks like one of the last people in the world who'd be writing stuff like this. Until you get to know her, with her long history of smut, dirty fanfic, and sex-in-gaming books/articles, not to mention her habit of mutilating -- I mean, customizing! -- Barbie dolls.

Picture by Erik Wilson

www.ingramcontent.com/pod-product-compliance
Lightning Source LLC
Chambersburg PA
CBHW051125260626
47170CB00005B/1669